TANGLED BY

Doms of Destiny, Colorado 7

Chloe Lang

MENAGE EVERLASTING

Siren Publishing, Inc.
www.SirenPublishing.com

A SIREN PUBLISHING BOOK
IMPRINT: Ménage Everlasting

TANGLED BY TEMPTATION
Copyright © 2014 by Chloe Lang

ISBN: 978-1-62741-370-1

First Printing: June 2014

Cover design by Les Byerley
All art and logo copyright © 2014 by Siren Publishing, Inc.

Printed in the U.S.A.

PUBLISHER
Siren Publishing, Inc.
www.SirenPublishing.com

DEDICATION

This one is for all the teachers. None of us would be able to read or write without you. Thank you for all you do!

TANGLED BY TEMPTATION

Doms of Destiny, Colorado 7

CHLOE LANG

Chapter One

Belle White looked down at her half-eaten lunch and tried to tamp down her desire and nervousness. Sitting at the burger joint between the two sexy brothers had her temperature rising fast.

Shane Blue put his hand on her thigh, delivering a delicious tingle. "Don't you like hamburgers?"

She smiled, never tiring of his touch and teasing.

"Don't you, sweetheart? Or should we have taken you somewhere else?" His brother Corey placed his hand on her other thigh, adding to her sweet discomfort.

She stifled a giggle. *This is so unlike me. Why am I acting like a silly teenager? Because they are making me so hot—that's why.*

"I love burgers, especially from here, but I had a large breakfast at the Boys Ranch, fellas. Bacon and eggs, biscuits and gravy."

Her sister Amber loved cooking, which was a good thing since there were so many mouths to feed at the ranch. Belle loved Amber. When she and Amber were teenagers, they'd lost both their parents to cancer and had become even closer. To this day, Amber was her very best friend.

"We'll have to let Lucy know you're finished with your lunch." Shane waved at the owner of Lucy's Burgers, who stood behind the counter.

The middle-aged woman was dressed in her 1950s pink waitress uniform, holding her signature hula hoop, wearing roller skates. Like most in Destiny, Lucy was sweet, quirky, and wonderful.

Corey ate his last French fry. "She'll wrap up the remainder of your burger in a to-go box for you."

"You can have the rest of mine if you'd like." Belle pushed her plate in front of him.

The way they took charge and were touching her thighs reminded her that they were in a lifestyle that several in Destiny practiced. Phase Four was a BDSM club many belonged to, including Amber and her three husbands. Though the idea of it intrigued her, she couldn't imagine walking into the place the way she looked. "If I keep eating these kind of meals, I'm going to put on the pounds. I'm already too fat."

Both men squeezed her legs, making her dizzy with want.

Keeping her control, her calm, and her cool was proving impossible.

Why had she agreed to another lunch date with Shane and Corey? Because her hot dreams about them were invading all her daytime thoughts. But she knew this couldn't go anywhere, at least anywhere serious.

Shane grinned, his blue eyes sparkling. His hair had grown out from the buzz cut he'd sported for the past three years, making his appearance even more handsome than ever. "Then I guess I'm into fat, Belle, if you want to call your beautiful body that, 'cause I'm definitely into you."

Corey's dark eyes locked in on her. "Don't put yourself down, sweetheart." God, he looked scrumptious in his US marshal uniform. "Belle, you're a beautiful woman."

You are beautiful, too, Corey. "Perhaps you should get your eyes checked, Mr. Blue. I'm average, slightly above average on good days in the looks department, but thank you."

"Oh boy." Shane smiled broadly and shook his head. "You don't want to set him off, Belle. My brother doesn't like to be questioned."

"Oh really? Not my problem." She grinned. Though she'd only been on a few dates with Shane and Corey, she would bet their tastes in women ran to the more subdued, submissive types. Not her at all. "I'm not someone who can be ordered around by men."

Corey put his arm around her shoulder. "Maybe you haven't been around the right men, Belle."

"That's for sure," Shane said. "Until now."

"A woman doesn't have much of a chance with you two." She shook her head. *This can't be anything more than fun and games. Nothing more.* "I need to get over to the Dream Hotel."

"That's right. Today is the big baking event for the Thanksgiving meal." Shane pushed his empty plate to the side. "I'm pretty good at making chocolate chip cookies. Maybe I could join you."

Corey laughed. "You're only good when it comes out of a pre-packaged tube, bro. Best to leave the baking to the experts. What are you making, Belle?"

"Apple pies. My mom's recipe. I've never made ten of them at the same time though." She missed her mom very much, as did Amber.

"I definitely want to have a slice at the meal."

"You better be early." Shane smacked his lips. His warm personality was endearing to her. "Maybe even first in line. Apple pie is a Destiny favorite. It'll be gone fast."

The whole town celebrated Thanksgiving together in the ballroom of the Dream Hotel. Destonians loved spending time together.

She'd come to adore the residents of this tiny Colorado town. "I hope people like mine."

"Oh my God, sweetheart." Corey looked into her eyes. It would be easy to lose herself in his hot gaze. "I'm sure everyone will love them."

"Especially Corey and me. I talked to Tad, the manager of the hotel. He's made sure that you get to sit between me and Corey, sweetheart."

Time to put a stop—

Interrupting her thoughts, a woman came through the front door and collapsed.

Being a nurse, Belle reacted quickly. "Let me out, Corey."

He nodded, sliding out of the booth.

"Call Doc Ryder, guys." She rushed to the woman on the floor. Corey remained at her side.

"I'll get a cold cloth." Lucy ran through the swinging door that led to the kitchen.

The unconscious woman's eyes were closed, but she was breathing steadily. She looked to be about Belle's age, which was twenty-eight.

Pulse? Normal.

Temperature? Also normal.

The woman's color looked fine, too.

"Doc, this is Shane Blue. We're over at Lucy's. A woman has passed out." He clicked off the phone and bent down next to Belle and Corey. "Doc's on his way. How is she?"

Belle kept her eyes on her patient, who sported dark hair, styled in the latest fashion in bob cuts. "I don't believe it's anything serious, but we'll need to wait for Doc Ryder to be sure."

Lucy handed her a damp cloth. "She's a pretty thing. Not from around here though. I wonder who she is?"

So did Belle. Strangers didn't show up in Destiny often. Of late, whenever one did they always brought trouble.

The woman came to, her brown eyes wide. "Where am I?"

"You're in Destiny, Colorado."

"Oh." She shifted, attempting to sit up. "I'm so confused. I was coming to Destiny, but how did I get here?"

"Stay put, please," Belle instructed. "You passed out. The doctor is on his way. I'm a nurse. Have you ever done this before?"

"No. I'm fine, just trying to get my bearings. I was in Twin Falls and now I'm here. Strange." The woman shook her head. "I might be a little dehydrated. I've been battling a stomach issue for a few days. That's all. Who are you?"

"I'm Belle White." She pointed to her two lunch dates. "They are Shane and Corey Blue."

"And I'm Lucy Little, the owner of this place."

"Pleased to meet all of you."

Lucy leaned forward. "Who are you, miss?"

"I'm Cindy."

Doc Ryder and his nurse Paris Cottrell, rushed in, followed by Doc's brother, Mick.

Corey stepped back. "You got here fast."

"We were only a few buildings away." Mick took off his black Stetson. "We were having lunch at Phong's."

Belle stepped back, making room for Doc and Paris. "Her vitals are normal, Doc. She came in and fainted. Cindy says she's been battling a stomach virus and might be dehydrated."

"Thanks, Belle." Doc opened his bag, pulling out a blood pressure cuff. "Let's see what your pressure is, Cindy."

"Shall I go get a bed set up for her, Doctor?" Paris's nursing skills were quite impressive. No wonder, since she had her Masters in the field. "She needs an IV as soon as possible."

"I know what she needs, Nurse." Doc's tone was harsh. "It's amazing what medical school will teach you."

Paris's face tightened as she placed a thermometer in Cindy's ear. "Ninety-eight point six."

Belle had gotten close to Paris, who had told her about the rift that had grown between her and Doc of late. Mick stood behind them. Belle, like most in town, knew these three belonged together. Paris had confessed to her she wasn't so sure. The two brothers were like night and day—Mick being a rancher and so easy-going and Doc being...well, Doc.

"Shall I go get the room set up or not, Doctor?" Paris asked sharply.

"Go," he ordered.

Everyone felt the tension between the two.

"I'll help you." Mick followed Paris out the door.

"Belle mentioned something about you being dehydrated. Tell me why."

"I haven't been able to keep anything down because I've been so nervous. That's why I passed out."

Belle grabbed her hand. "What are you nervous about?"

"It's a long story." Cindy smiled and squeezed her hand. She turned to Doc Ryder. "I'm feeling much better, Doctor. May I sit up now?"

"Your pressure is perfect. Sure."

The woman sat up, handing the cloth back to Lucy. "Thank you. Thank you all for your kindness."

Lucy grinned, handing Cindy a glass of water. "That's how Destiny rolls, miss. No trouble at all."

She took a sip. "I'm fine now."

"Like Paris said, we need to get you started on an IV." Doc turned to Shane and Corey. "Will you two help me get her to the clinic? I want to make sure she doesn't pass out on the way."

"Sure." Something in Shane's gaze on Cindy seemed to hold back a warm welcome for the new arrival. What was going through his mind?

"We'll be happy to help you, Doc." Corey looked at Cindy. He didn't seem polite or neighborly either. "Exactly who are you?"

"Perhaps I should start with why I'm here," she answered. "I need your help."

"Yes, you do." Doc assisted her to her feet. "That's what I'm here for."

"Thank you, but I'm not talking about medical help, Doctor. I came here for another reason."

"And that is?" Shane's tone was full of accusation, surprising Belle.

"That can wait, Mr. Blue." Lucy placed her hands on her hips, emphasizing she meant business. "She needs to get to the clinic, like Doc and Paris said."

Cindy shook her head. "Really, I'm fine now."

"Maybe so." Doc placed the blood pressure cuff back in his bag. "But you aren't going anywhere until I get you fully checked out. You're under my care now until I release you. Understand?"

"Okay."

"What are you doing in Destiny, Cindy?"

"I'm hoping someone can help me. There's a madman after me. I'm terrified, but I need to tell you who I am. I'm afraid what you'll think of me when I do."

Corey leaned forward. "Who are you?"

"I'm Cindy Trollinger. Kip Lunceford is my brother."

Belle felt her heart skip several beats.

Kip Lunceford, the murdering, brilliant madman who had declared war on Destiny.

Chapter Two

"We've been expecting you, Miss Trollinger." Shane looked directly into Kip Lunceford's sister's eyes for any sign of deceit.

"You have, Mr. Blue?" Her responses all appeared genuine. She shared the same DNA as the master manipulator, so Shane couldn't be sure it wasn't all just an act.

Belle looked surprised, too. "Really?"

He nodded, pulling her protectively to his side away from Cindy. Yes, Trollinger looked harmless, but he knew very well that looks were often deceiving.

Shannon's Elite, the CIA black ops team he and Corey were members of, had been briefed about Lunceford's sister's pending arrival a couple of weeks earlier.

Doc motioned to him and Corey. "Let's get her over to the clinic."

Of course, the "clinic" wasn't an actual clinic at all. Fire had destroyed the original one, and the new one was still being built. Doc and team were operating out of the county courthouse for the time being.

"Will do." Shane got on one side of Cindy, placing his arm around her waist to support her. He didn't buy her story. Not one damn bit. He tightened his hold, just in case she tried to make a move. "Belle, you stay here until we get back." He didn't want her around Kip's sister until they had her secure.

"Not happening, cowboy." Belle's fire was something he liked, liked very much. But he couldn't let his desires for her get in the way of what he had to do. Not now. Not this close to someone who was connected to Kip Lunceford, the Agency's Most Wanted. He needed to remain focused.

Corey moved to the other side of the woman. "I'll be right here, Miss Trollinger, to back up Shane. We won't let you fall."

"Please, call me Cindy."

Lucy held the door for them. "I'll box up your leftovers and put them in the fridge."

"You don't have to do that," Belle said.

"But I will."

They walked Kip's sister out of Lucy's Burgers. Doc and Belle followed behind.

Cindy looked at him straight in the eyes. "I really can walk on my own."

"I'm certain you can, but the Doc asked me to help you. That's exactly what I am going to do."

Whatever evil you and Kip have cooked up, I'm not going to let you get away with it.

If her story turned out to be true and she was innocent, he still would prepare himself for the worst. Like it or not, she had a connection to Lunceford. She was either working with him or in danger of him. Whichever it was, the team would need to keep her under guard.

"This is a lovely town." Her words infuriated him.

Destiny was his home. "Just keep putting one foot in front of the other."

She nodded.

He recalled how he'd learned about Cindy Trollinger.

Still trying to track down Lunceford, Easton Black, the leader of Shannon's Elite, had told the entire team about Miss Trollinger. The existence of Lunceford's sister had been unknown until recently, when a data mining exercise back at Langley had uncovered several Internet searches by the woman looking for Kip. Digging deeper, they discovered records of Trollinger's adoption. Apparently, Kip's father had cheated on his wife, producing a child several years younger than her half brother.

As they crossed South Street to the corner of the park where one of the four dragon statues sat, Cindy smiled. "Thank you for helping me."

"What's the last thing you remember?" he asked her.

"I was driving to Destiny. I stopped in Twin Falls, Idaho to stretch my legs and get a drink. Then I woke up here."

He glanced over at Corey, who was clearly having as difficult a time believing Cindy's story as he was. The rest of the trek to the courthouse was done in silence.

Being undercover in a federal prison for three years had taught Shane to trust his instincts before anything else, and his instincts right now didn't trust a fucking thing that was coming out of the woman's mouth.

Just as they'd discovered Cindy's existence, she'd gone missing. For a week. The only reason they knew she had been headed to Destiny was because of the traces the team had placed on her phone and e-mail accounts the very first day.

They entered the room that Paris had gotten ready for Miss Trollinger. It had the latest and greatest medical equipment, thanks to the very generous donations of the local billionaire families in town.

Paris helped Cindy to the bed. "We've got it from here, Shane. You and Corey wait outside until we get her settled in."

"Belle is coming with us." Corey wasn't giving any room for argument.

"I'm a nurse. Paris might be glad to have my help."

Shane put his arm around her shoulder, unwilling to leave her alone with Trollinger. "Who said our date was over?"

Paris smiled. "Go out in the hallway with them, Belle."

Doc nodded, checking Cindy's vitals again. "We've got it covered now."

Belle shrugged. "Okay."

Shane felt his shoulders relax some, but only some.

He, Belle, and Corey went into the hallway.

Belle's eyelids narrowed, hiding much of her mesmerizing green orbs. "What's with you two?"

Taking time to appreciate how gorgeous she was didn't fit the current situation. But even though his guard was up, he did let his gaze linger on her for a little longer than he should have. God, she was something to behold. The whole package. Flaxen hair, soft to the touch. She had the body of a real woman, curves and all. He and Corey knew she had never been to Phase Four and that she had never been in the life. It didn't matter to him or his brother. First, they needed to make her their own. Later, they could introduce her to the life.

He looked her straight in the eyes. "What do you mean?"

"Fine. Don't tell me. I just don't understand why you were being so...so rude to Cindy."

"How were we rude?" Corey asked. "We helped her get here from Lucy's, didn't we?"

"Yes, but the look on both your faces was unmistakable to me. You don't care for her. Just because she's related to Lunceford doesn't mean she's like him."

"It also doesn't mean she isn't, Belle." Shane still found it hard to believe that Kip's sister was actually on the run from him. He would need more than just the woman's word to be convinced otherwise, and so would the rest of Shannon's Elite.

Corey leaned against the now closed door to Cindy's room. "She's been on the team's list for some time. We believe she could be the key to finding Kip."

Hearing Corey open up so freely with Belle about Agency business was strange to Shane, though Black's new team wasn't covert like he'd been.

"I don't trust her." Shane fired off a text on his ROC, the encrypted Agency device, to the rest of the team. They would all want to know about Trollinger.

Belle shook her head. "Whatever happened to innocent until proven guilty?"

"That's in court, sweetheart. The Agency rarely has to deal with the justice system."

Her green eyes locked in on him. "I can only imagine."

He needed to get her away from here, away from Trollinger. "Shouldn't you be headed to the hotel to bake? I'll be happy to take you."

"Going to be quite the event," Corey added, clearly on the same page about hoping to get Belle to leave.

"Like I said, you two are acting so weird. No. I'm staying. The baking party will have to start without me."

Paris opened the door. "You may come in now."

They walked into the room. He made certain to remain next to Belle and to keep his hand within a fraction of an inch from his Glock. He immediately noticed something that added to his misgivings. "Doc, no IV? I thought she was dehydrated."

"A little, but nothing to worry about. I think she fainted because of stress more than anything else, but I want to keep her here under observation for the night."

"Is your patient up for some questions?" Corey asked.

Doc nodded. He, too, knew the risk of her being in Destiny and also being Kip's only living flesh and blood. "But it's up to her whether to answer you or not."

"I'm happy to answer any questions you have for me."

"You were contacted by a friend of mine, Miss Trollinger. Mr. Black. Do you remember him?"

"Yes. I do. He's with the government, right?"

"He is." Shane continued studying Cindy's demeanor, looking for any clue she might be lying, but so far he hadn't discovered any.

Black had sent agents to her home in Idaho, but had found the place empty. When they'd checked with her boss about her whereabouts, he told them she'd resigned, saying she had personal issues she wanted to work through. She'd only been at the job for a few weeks. Very suspicious. "I'm sure you have a ton of questions for

Mr. Black about your brother."

"I do." She sighed. "I read everything I could about Kip on the Internet. I guess you all know what kind of things he's done, don't you?"

"Yes, we do." Corey rubbed his chin, a sure sign that he was still on the fence about whether to believe the woman's story or not. "What brings you to Destiny, Miss Trollinger?"

"I'm not my brother, you understand. I've read so much about him." Her hands began to tremble. "You can imagine how shocked and horrified I was. Sharing his blood sickens me."

"That still doesn't answer the question, Miss Trollinger." Shane remembered the e-mail the team had discovered that Cindy had sent to her cleaning lady. Trollinger had told the woman she was headed to Destiny. "Just why are you here? Who are you looking for? Your brother? He isn't here. Perhaps you could shed some light on his whereabouts."

"I can't. I have no idea where Kip is, but I'm here because he has been sending me messages, saying he wants to meet me. I'm terrified, of course. I didn't know where to turn." Cindy's eyes welled up. "I came to Destiny to find Mr. Black. He is here, isn't he? That's what his message said."

Belle nodded. "Yes, he lives in Destiny now."

"But he's away," Corey informed. "He'll be back tonight."

"Please. I need to talk to him. I need his help. Kip is a monster. We have to find him. We have to stop him."

Shane pulled Belle in tighter. "Why should we believe you, Miss Trollinger? Why would a sister turn on her brother?"

"I never knew I had a brother. I don't know him. I don't want to know him. He's a killer." The woman wiped her eyes. "He's a monster. Please. I need your help."

Still no sign of deceit. She was either telling the truth or an incredible actress.

Do I trust my gut on this?

* * * *

"What kind of help, Miss Trollinger, do you want from us?" Looking down at Kip's sister, Corey wondered how much truth the woman was telling them.

"Check my purse. I received a letter from Kip. He knows about me and that scares me to death. Belle, would you mind getting it out and reading it for everyone?"

"Sure thing."

She nodded and started to step forward, but he blocked her. "I'll get it for you."

Even though Cindy was in a hospital bed, he didn't want Belle any closer to her than she was.

He grabbed the purse from the side table where it had been placed and handed it to Belle.

She reached in and pulled out an envelope. "Are you sure you want me to read it, Cindy?"

"Yes, Belle. I trust you. Mr. Black, Shane, and Corey are my only hope."

Before Belle could begin reading the letter, Jason Wolfe, the sheriff of Destiny, and Dylan Strange, who never was without his sunglasses, walked into the room. They were two other members of Shannon's Elite.

"Shane, I got your text and brought Dylan with me." Jason walked over to the bed. "Miss Trollinger, I have a few questions for you."

"Hold on, Sheriff." Belle's traits of protectiveness, caring, and kindness were in full force for Cindy.

Corey wasn't sure they were warranted now. He and Shane had witnessed Belle's wonderful motherly instincts firsthand with all the orphans that were already at the Boys Ranch, but especially with Juan.

God, she was the perfect woman for him and Shane, but the timing wasn't right for a serious relationship.

Shane was obviously moving too fast. He'd only just gotten released from prison. Even though Corey could see them eventually going forward with her to see where it might lead, he knew they needed to keep it casual for now. Belle had made it clear that's what she wanted, too. In another year or so, maybe then he and Shane could get more serious with her, but not before.

"Belle, I only want to talk to Miss Trollinger," Jason said. "She might have some information that would help us find her brother. That's all."

"She's already been answering a ton of questions, Sheriff. I'm about to read a letter she got from her brother that she wants us all to hear."

"Read on," Dylan said.

Belle nodded and began reading.

Dear Cynthia,

Let me introduce myself. I am your brother.

I know that may come as a shock to you, but I am. Knowing my bastard father gave you up for adoption is something I can't even get my head around.

I have no family. You're the only one left. I ask you to keep this letter secret because there are people looking for me. Yes, I've done some terrible things in my life. If you do a Google search, you'll see tons of write-ups about me—some true, most exaggerated.

I'm sorry for all the wrongs I've done, but believe me, I'm a changed person now.

To prove my intentions are pure, I've left a present for you. Enclosed is a key to a mailbox at a UPS location in Seattle. Your gift is inside. I wish I could've brought it to you or gotten it closer to your home, but things are a little difficult at the moment for me.

I've also attached the directions to the store and number of the box.

I want to meet you. When the time is right, I will come to you.

Looking forward to meeting you in person.
Love,
Your brother,
Kip

Cindy looked visibly shaken. "So you see why I came to see Mr. Black. I'm terrified Kip will find me."

Corey knew the woman's letter might just be the lead the team needed to capture Kip. Was the bastard really in Seattle?

Chapter Three

Belle sipped her wine, taking a break from peeling apples. Her hand was beginning to ache. Thank God, she had a team of helpers that had been assigned by the two women who were in charge of the event. The matriarchs of the town, both in their eighties, were the sweetest women she'd ever known.

Gretchen Hollingsworth, being a miracle worker in the kitchen, was the lead today. Ethel O'Leary, known for throwing the best parties, would be in charge tomorrow of the Thanksgiving meal.

Gretchen, carrying a clipboard, came over to her station. "Are these dear girls doing a good job for you, Belle?"

She nodded, looking at the three young women that had been recruited from Destiny High. "They are doing a wonderful job. They are the best apple peelers in the county and deserve a blue ribbon."

The girls smiled broadly.

"That's great. How are you doing on time?"

"We're about done peeling the apples. I'll start them on making the crusts next."

Gretchen looked down at her notes. "Your pies are scheduled for ovens three and four at five sharp."

"We'll be ready, won't we, girls?"

"Yes," the trio said in unison.

Gretchen smiled and went to the next station, where the pumpkin pies were being made. Betty Anderson and her daughter Kaylyn were in charge of more high school girls who were helping.

"Girls, I'm going to stretch my legs. You finish up and come get me when you're done."

"We will, Miss White." Rylie Gold was a senior at the high school and the daughter of Zac Gold. She was quite a beauty and quite charming. Mr. Gold was a single parent who was clearly doing a wonderful job with Rylie.

Belle grabbed her wine and walked around the Dream Hotel's kitchen.

At the chocolate cake station, Jena Dixon-MacCabe and her mom were surrounded by a group of students, including Jena's five-year-old daughter, Kimmie.

At other stations around the kitchen were women who had become friends to Belle. Jennifer Steele, owner of Steele Ranch, and Phoebe Blue, fiancée to the Wolfe brothers and sister to Shane and Corey, were in charge of the brownies. Megan Knight, Nicole Coleman, and Erica Strange were tackling Belle's least favorite dessert. Minced Meat Pie. *Yuck.*

You should've been here by now, Amber. Where are you?

Belle was anxious to talk to her sister about what had happened with Shane and Corey. It was clear that things were moving to something more serious than she wanted.

Amber and two of her three husbands were busy with the plans for the official opening of the Boys Ranch, which was a week before Christmas. More orphan boys would be arriving then, and the dorms had to be completed. Juan was so excited.

My sweet Juan.

He and the other boys were on another dragon hunting quest with Cody Stone, Amber's most playful spouse. Belle loved all the boys, but especially Juan. He'd been with her the longest. In Chicago, Amber had brought him to her after discovering a drug dealer was using him.

Covered in flour, Paris walked up to her. "You look like something is on your mind. Everything okay?"

Belle loved all the women in Destiny, but especially Paris, whom she'd grown extremely close to. "All good. About to get the girls on making crusts. How's it going with you?"

"I'm not that good in the kitchen, but thankfully, I'm not the only woman helping the girls at the cookie station. But I wasn't talking about the baking. You're wondering about Kip's sister and if her story is true, aren't you?"

"You sound like Shane and Corey. Why shouldn't we believe her?"

"Because she's Kip's sister, that's why. You and I both know—hell, the whole town knows—what kind of man he is. That letter you read doesn't make any sense to me. Who writes letters today? No one, and definitely not someone like Kip, who is a genius when it comes to computers. Why wouldn't he have sent her an e-mail or text message?"

"I did think that was strange, but that still doesn't mean Cindy is lying. She seems so sweet. Didn't you notice how shaken she was after I read the letter?"

Paris smiled. "You might be a stickler about rules and tough on the outside, Belle, but you have a very soft heart. You want to believe the best about everyone."

"Why not? Most people are good inside. That's what I believe."

"Just be on your guard in case you're wrong, okay?" Paris pointed behind her. "Your sister just arrived."

She turned around and saw Amber being greeted by several women.

"I just heard the good news. When's your baby due, Amber?" one of them from nearby Clover asked.

"June eleventh," her sister answered. "I can't wait to be a mother."

Gretchen walked over to Amber and told her where she was assigned.

Belle was thrilled about the new baby. She and Amber had already painted the nursery a pale green. She couldn't wait to hold the tiny bundle in her arms. The pending arrival of the newest member of the family also reminded her of her own heartbreak and loss. She'd finally come to accept the reality of what she couldn't change about herself.

After Gretchen moved on to her next baking station, Amber spotted Belle.

She waved her over.

"I better get back to the cookies," Paris said. "I'm going to the clinic to check on Cindy after we've finished baking. If you want, you could go with me."

"I definitely want to. You and I could grab a bite at the diner after. I bet you could use a friendly ear, too."

Paris sighed. "Yes, I could. Doc won't let up on trying to get me to apply to medical school. He can be such an ass."

"I think he has your best interests at heart, even if he goes about it in the wrong way."

"Maybe." Paris gave her a little wave as she went back to her station.

Amber stepped up. "Hey, Belle."

"They have apple juice for all the pregnant women, Sis. You want some?"

"I'm fine."

Belle needed her sister right now more than ever. "Can we talk?"

"Sure. Gretchen told me I'm on cookie icing duty, which will be starting in about thirty minutes. Is that enough time?"

"Plenty." She led her sister to the banquet room, which was already set up with tables and chairs for tomorrow's event. "Let's sit here."

"I can tell you're upset, Sis." Amber always could read her better than anyone. "I got your text about Kip's sister. Is that what's troubling you? Is she still at the courthouse?"

"She is, and that's part of what I want to talk about."

"I'm sure Black's team will keep her safe."

"Shane and Corey don't trust the poor girl. I understand their skepticism, but I want to give her the benefit of the doubt just like Mom and Dad taught us."

"Yes, they did teach us that, Belle, but they never knew someone like Kip even existed. I think we should be cautious around Cindy for the time being. You always lead with your heart first, which is why I love you so much, but this time, please lead with your head. Okay?"

"That's what I'm trying to do when it comes to Shane and Corey. You should've seen them. They treated me as if I was made of glass. Once we found out Cindy's identity, they both kept trying, not so subtly, to keep me away from her as if she could've hurt me in her condition. Really, Sis, it was totally ridiculous. I don't need protection. If anyone needs to be guarded, it is Cindy. Kip told her in the letter that he was coming to meet her."

"I bet Jason will make sure she is watched over. About Shane and Corey being overprotective…that's how the men of Destiny operate. I've had to get used to it with Emmett, Cody, and Bryant. You will, too."

"You want me to act like a princess waiting for her knights in shining armor to come rescue her?" She grinned. "You know me better than that. I'm the one who wants to slay the dragon."

"Hush," Amber said, looking around the empty room. "You never know who might be listening. If Patrick heard you say that, he'd bring you up on charges."

Belle laughed. "I know. Okay, I would slay whatever monster showed up. You know what I mean. I'm self-sufficient. Always have been. That's the way I like it."

"I know better. Yes, you're strong. You've always been the best sister and have always been there for me. Now, it's my turn to give you some tough love." Amber smiled. "When it comes to Shane and Corey, I think your heart needs to be first, not the other way around."

"They are wonderfully exciting gentlemen. I've been so at ease until recently. It seems they both like me, and I definitely like them."

"That's a good thing, right?"

"I suppose so. I've been having fun, but I think Shane wants to take it to the next level, which you and I both know I can't do."

"I don't know why, Belle."

"Of course you do. You know everything about me, Amber. You know my entire history." Belle felt the old sting bubble up inside her. "You know what happened with Stan."

"Doctor Asshole? The man with the gambling addiction? Yes. I know what happened. You dodged a bullet."

"Losing him was hard, but it wasn't what broke my heart. That relationship was clearly doomed from the very beginning."

"He's the jerk who pushed you to the curb when you needed him most. He's a bastard, Belle. I'm glad you're not with him anymore. You deserve better."

"Have you forgotten why we broke it off?"

"Yes, because he's a self-centered dick, that's why."

She couldn't help but grin. Amber always had her back, especially in her darkest time. "That's true, but I really can't blame him. We both wanted kids. What crushed me was the fact that I couldn't have children."

Amber grabbed her hands. "It still could happen, Belle."

She shook her head. "With my endometriosis, the odds are better for me winning the lottery than getting pregnant. I've had the surgery. I've done the hormones. I've done everything medicine has to offer. Nothing. It's never going to happen, Amber. Even though I've accepted that fact, I'm still dealing with it. I think about it every day. Having Juan in my life has softened much of the hurt. He's my boy. I love him with all my heart. I'm ready to pursue adopting him, though I know it will be difficult being a single woman."

"Have you told Shane and Corey? They clearly are fond of Juan, too. Don't they deserve the chance to tell you if whether you can have their children or not makes any difference to them? They might be just as happy adopting."

She shook her head. "Why should I tell them now? Don't you

think it's way too early for that kind of conversation? Let's just say I go down the relationship highway with them until I can bring up my illness. Even if they told me it didn't matter, I would know it really did."

"You can't know that, Belle. You aren't a mind reader."

"But I do know it. Besides, it still matters to me. I will not take away anyone's chance at having a child."

"Does that mean you are only going to get serious with men past their prime, men who have already had children with other women?"

"I hadn't thought about it, but that isn't a bad idea. Maybe I wait until I'm forty before I put myself out there for a serious relationship." Belle laughed like she always did when trying to hide her pain. "A little gray hair, a few more pounds, some wrinkles. That way any man who would date me would know what they were getting into."

"I never thought you would be such a chicken, Belle. Where's my tough sister, the one who put herself through nursing school waiting tables on the graveyard shift?"

"I'm still that *tough* sister, Amber." She didn't feel that tough, but hoped it didn't show. "That's why I'm making this *tough* decision."

Chapter Four

Standing in a recently vacated part of TBK's headquarters, Corey entered his security code into a keypad.

"Welcome, agent." The computerized voice from the hidden speaker sounded British, which amused him. "Place your right hand on the pad for final verification."

He did, and the door to Shannon's Elite's temporary offices opened.

In the high-tech conference room were some of the other members of the team around the long glass table.

Dylan sat next to Jason and Nicole Coleman, Jason's deputy sheriff.

Jena, the talented hacker, sat across from them with her husbands, Sean MacCabe and Matt Dixon.

"Shane's not with you?" Dylan always did get right to the point.

Corey shook his head. "Black assigned him to guard duty for Kip's sister for the time being."

"I bet we'll all get a crack at guard duty as long as Trollinger remains in town." He couldn't agree more with Jason's assessment.

"Black will not trust anyone but his own agents to guard her," Dylan stated flatly.

Sean put his arm around Jena. "I doubt Black will let the woman leave until we get our hands on Lunceford."

"You're right about that, Mr. MacCabe." Black walked into the conference room with Joanne Brown, his second in command of the team. "Cindy Trollinger is our best chance at capturing Kip Lunceford. Have a seat Corey. There's much to discuss."

"You can say that again, boss. Shane and I were there when Kip's sister passed out at Lucy's." He recalled how quickly Belle had reacted to help her and just as quickly had been ready to accept her story on its face. He loved how trusting Belle was, but it also worried him. "I don't have a good feeling about this Cindy woman, boss."

"Can you expand on that for us, please?" Black asked.

"I think that fainting spell was all a ruse. I can't put my finger on it, but according to Belle, Doc, and Paris, her vitals were normal. The fact that Cindy got inside the restaurant before she fainted seems quite strange to me." He took a seat next to Dylan. "There's got to be more to this."

"I'm sure there is. That's why you are all on my team. I trust your instincts." Black sat at the head of the table. "I understand we have a good lead that came from the letter Miss Trollinger brought with her."

"Who has the letter?" Brown moved next to Nicole.

"I have the original. I also made a digital copy for everyone." Dylan activated his ROC. "Check your secure files. Lunceford could be in Seattle."

Corey looked at the copy on his screen, even though he had listened to Belle read it at the clinic. Could it really be the key to Kip's true location?

After everyone finished scanning the letter, Black nodded. "We can't accept this on face value. This could be just another of Lunceford's grand schemes. I'll contact my counterpart in Seattle and have him send some operatives to this UPS store to retrieve whatever is in that box. Miss Trollinger must remain under guard. Whether she's telling the truth or not, which remains to be seen, Kip is clearly interested in her."

"We've checked her background," Jo said. "So far, everything points to her story being true."

"Check it again."

"Matt, Sean, and I can dig deeper into Trollinger's records." Jena typed something into her ROC. "We're very familiar with Kip's digital fingerprints. If he's tampered with them in anyway, we will know."

"Perfect," Easton said. "Jo, you get with our counterparts at Langley and let them know this new development."

"On it, sir."

"Right now, Shane is outside Trollinger's room. I'm talking with Doc Ryder about the situation after this meeting." Easton always had all of his thoughts in strategic order. "I think we should have two agents with her at all times."

"Sounds like a plan." Jason had incredible drive and a passion for right and wrong that had always impressed Corey. "I can head there right now."

"What do we do after Doc releases her?" Nicole's question had merit. She was a terrific agent.

"I'm going to ask the good doctor to keep Miss Trollinger a few more days until we can decide what our next steps are and verify her story." Easton looked at his watch. "It's 2:15. Jason, you and Shane finish the first shift. Let's go eight hours for now. If we need to expand that, we can later. Dylan and Nicole take the next one at ten. Corey and Jo will be on at six in the morning. I know tomorrow is the big Thanksgiving meal. I'll fill in the gaps so everyone can get a good dinner."

Sean leaned forward. "Matt and I can start up the next shift after that."

"Not yet. I need you two and Jena working on the system round the clock. Find a way to keep that bastard out." He motioned to Jo. "Time to introduce everyone to our new team members."

"Yes, sir."

"New members?" Corey wondered how big the Agency wanted this team to be.

"Our mission has been expanded, Marshall." As three faces appeared on the large monitor on the wall, Easton continued. "Although Lunceford remains our main target at this point, we are now tasked with fighting a wider variety of international cyber terrorism, with special focus on the former Soviet Union. Let me introduce you to your newest team members, agents Brock Grayson, Cooper Ross, and Jonas Ward. Welcome, gentlemen, to Shannon's Elite."

Their images flickered and then turned to static.

Suddenly, a face they all knew very well filled the screen.

Kip Lunceford glared at them with his soulless eyes. "Hello, Shannon's Elite. I know you have my sister."

Jason and Dylan jumped to their feet.

Jo was frantically punching the keys to her ROC. "How the hell did he get past our security?"

Kip's lips curled into a hideous grin. "Jena's hurdles were quite impressive and a bit of a challenge, Agent Brown. But I finally got through them. I'm that good."

Corey saw Sean, Matt, and Jena working away on their devices, clearly trying to trace the bastard's location.

"Lunceford, I'm prepared to offer you a deal," Easton said calmly. "Are you ready to talk?"

"I know you're just stalling to try to give your little trio tech team a chance to find me. Won't happen. The maze I put up would take them hours to crack. Now, shut up, Black, and listen. As I said before, I know you have my sister. Trust me. You won't for long."

"It's our understanding that you two have never met," Easton said.

"What does that matter? She's my sister, my family, my blood. Don't you dare harm her or you will suffer. It's in your best interest to back off. I'm coming to get her and there is not a fucking thing you can do to stop me. Haven't you learned by now that I'm smarter than all of you?"

The screen went dark.

Easton looked at Sean. "Anything?"

The Texan shook his head. "He was telling the truth about the maze he set up."

"And it's already collapsing and shutting down." Matt sighed.

"He's gone."

"I recorded his transmission on my ROC." Jena continued to impress all of them. "I think we might be able to use something inside it that can help. Yes. Here it is. Though I can't give you the exact location, it did originate from the state of Washington."

Easton nodded. "Good work, agent."

Sean and Matt beamed with pride for their wife.

"We might actually get the bastard." Nicole voiced what they all were clearly hoping.

Cindy's letter was proving to be more valuable than any of them imagined.

Jason stood. "Time for me to get to my guard duty."

Easton nodded. "Once Grayson, Ross, and Ward get to town, we'll reassign the shifts. I know you and Nicole have other duties to attend to."

"Nothing is more important than capturing that motherfucker." All of them felt the same way as Jason. "My duty as sheriff is to make sure everyone is safe in Swanson County. Guarding his sister is part of it right now."

"Since Kip has cracked our systems again, let's go dark with all our communications. Face to face only from here on. With any luck, whatever Kip's gift to Cindy is will lead us straight to him." Easton turned to the tech trio. "You have any ideas about keeping Lunceford out?"

"We do, but it will take time," Jena said.

"Make it so."

"And please, as fast as possible," Jo added.

"We'll meet back here in twenty-four hours unless something happens before then. You are dismissed."

Corey's gut tightened as an image of Belle helping Trollinger at Lucy's appeared in his mind.

Kip Lunceford was coming to Destiny. They didn't know when, but they all knew he was.

Corey didn't want to be too far from Belle ever, so he headed straight to the big baking event at the Dream Hotel.

* * * *

Belle hurriedly went up the courthouse steps with Paris. "I hope your patient is feeling better."

"I'm sure she is." Paris walked through the large wooden doors. "You saw her vitals. It's weird she passed out, don't you think?"

"I wouldn't rule out anything yet." She nodded. Cindy's temperature, color, heartbeat, and respiration had been perfect, though she had seemed a little disoriented. "Did Doc run a blood test?"

"Yes. We should have the results shortly."

They walked into the grand entry of the Swanson County Courthouse. The building was over one hundred years old. The floors were a rich marble and the walls were a pale gray. Ornate dark oak doors and molding lined the space.

They turned down the hallway that led to the temporary clinic and hospital rooms.

Shane sat in a chair next to Cindy's door appearing more serious than Belle had ever seen him before. "Hello, ladies."

"Hi." Belle felt a shiver run up her spine as their eyes locked.

"Surely, the baking isn't over yet." Shane stood, his intense gaze never leaving hers.

"Could you move aside, soldier?" Paris had a job to do and, being a good nurse, was obviously not willing to be kept from it.

"For you, yes. You're Trollinger's nurse." What did he mean by that?

"Do you think you have a right to keep me from going in, Shane?" Belle folded her arms over her chest. He had no idea how stubborn she could be, but he was about to find out. "I'm here to assist Paris. So if you don't mind, we'd like to check on Cindy."

He hesitated, remaining between them and the door.

"I'm a nurse, too. I can help. Let me do my job." She could see in his face that he was torn about allowing her in. Did she need to tell him that she knew how to take care of herself? "Shane, please."

"You're a nurse and a very caring person, sweetheart." He grabbed her hand and squeezed, causing her to tingle all over. "I'll be right outside if you need me." He reluctantly stepped aside.

"Thank you." She and Paris walked into Cindy's room.

"Hi, Belle." Cindy was sitting up in bed. She looked perfectly fine—*and harmless.*

Is she?

* * * *

Shane felt uneasy allowing Belle to go inside Kip's sister's hospital room.

Ever since Cindy Trollinger's arrival in town, his gut screamed that something was wrong, very wrong.

He still didn't trust the woman.

There were several reasons why he had given in to Belle's request, though he would have preferred she remain in the hallway with him as Paris went inside.

One, he'd already checked Kip's sister's purse when she was asleep. No weapons.

Two, he knew there were no exit windows or doors inside the room. Anyone who wanted to get to Belle would have to go through him.

Three, her damn gorgeous eyes.

Four, her delicious curves.

Five, her caring heart.

Six, her fire and sass.

And a ton more reasons that kept him from refusing her anything.

He heard footsteps headed his way. By the sounds of the footfalls he knew they came from three men. He placed his hand on his gun, bracing himself.

Once the trio came into view at the end of the hallway, he relaxed.

Jason walked up to him. "Everything okay?"

"Quiet so far." Shane turned to his boss. "Belle and Paris are inside with her now. Sir, I am not sure we should trust Trollinger."

Easton nodded. "At the moment, we don't have any evidence to disprove anything she's told us. For now, let's just stay alert, Shane."

"I'm going to be on guard duty with you, buddy. Black has assigned us eight-hour shifts. You should be able to enjoy some of Thanksgiving with Belle tomorrow." Jason, like the entire town, knew he and Corey were dating her. One thing about Destiny, everyone here believed in love and romance.

"Shane, you said Paris was inside, too?" Doc asked.

He nodded.

"I don't want my nurse alone with the patient until we know for sure that Trollinger's story is proven to be true."

"I agree." Shane couldn't shake the feeling that there was much more to Cindy's arrival in town than any of them knew. "You know that Belle and Paris will think we're all being overprotective."

"So?" Doc turned to Easton. "I want them safe. Period."

"You got it. There's more news, Shane." He told him about Kip breaking through the security and taking over the video transmission.

Shane's frustration mounted. How were they going to catch the brilliant psychopath? "That means he's been on to our every move."

"The good news is Jena was able to narrow down the origination point of Kip's transmission to the state of Washington."

"Could he actually be in Seattle like the letter said?" Shane began to wonder if his first instinct about Cindy was wrong. Maybe she was completely innocent and telling the truth.

"As we speak there are agents going to check the box there and see what Kip left for his sister." Easton sighed. "We're going to go dark on all communications for now. ROCs are offline. Not ideal but necessary. Verbal only until Sean, Matt, and Jena come up with a new way to keep Lunceford out. Langley is heightening their security, too." Easton turned back to Doc. "Will you be able to help us with this mission and keep Miss Trollinger here for a few more days?"

"Yes. I still want to run some tests on her." Doc stared at the closed door. "None of us are sure that my patient is or is not telling the truth. Knowing what we do about Lunceford, he might've drugged her with something that made her pass out. I should be getting the results from the blood test any minute."

Jason shook his head. "The woman says she's never met her brother."

"When has that stopped Lunceford?" Shane wasn't sure Trollinger had been drugged, but ruling it out would help them get closer to the real truth.

They all turned as another set of footsteps echoed off the marble floors.

Corey appeared, his face tight with worry. "Where is Belle?"

Shane knew that he and his brother were in total agreement about the situation. He opened the door, unwilling to let another second pass without making sure both Belle and Paris were safe, especially Belle. "Inside."

* * * *

Belle was startled when the door opened and in charged Shane and Corey, followed by Doc, Jason, and Mr. Black.

"How's my patient?" Doc walked over to Paris.

"She's doing well." Paris handed him Cindy's chart.

Shane and Corey came up to Belle, one on each side. Corey put his arm around her shoulder and Shane grabbed her hand.

Only three dates and they were already acting like she was in something permanent with them, something more serious than it actually was, something it could never be.

Lead with your head, Belle, not your heart.

Easier said than done. Shane and Corey might have been quite overprotective of late, but she definitely liked being the center of their attention.

Why were Jason, Corey, and Mr. Black here? Did they have news about Cindy's brother?

Belle kept her eyes on Cindy, looking for any sign that Shane and Corey might be correct about her. They didn't trust her.

Were they right or could this woman, Kip's sister, be trusted? Belle wasn't ready to make the judgment just yet, still remaining cautious. So far, there'd been nothing to make her doubt Cindy, who seemed, at least on the outside, very kind.

Was it only an act? She just didn't know.

Doc listened to Cindy's heart through his stethoscope. "Quite the ticker, Miss Trollinger."

"I really am fine, doctor." Cindy's eyes were wide. She turned to Mr. Black. "I've met Corey, Shane, and the sheriff, but who are you?"

"You know me, too, Miss Trollinger, though we've never met face to face. I'm Easton Black." He extended his hand to her.

Cindy smiled, shaking his hand. "Pleased to meet you, Mr. Black. You can't imagine how thankful I am that you are here. I guess you've been told about the letter I received from Kip."

Belle noticed Cindy's lips begin to tremble. She seemed honestly frightened.

"I have. I'm assigning several agents to guard you, at least two a shift." Easton turned to Shane and Jason. "These are the two men who will be just outside your door for the first shift."

The smiling face Belle had come to expect on Shane wasn't there. In its place was a serious look that spoke volumes. It was clear he would keep any attackers away from the woman, but would also keep an eye on Cindy in case she turned out to be a threat as well.

"Thank you, Mr. Black, but will you mind if I move to the hotel? Can they guard me there?"

"Eventually we can set up something at the hotel for you, Miss Trollinger, but for now, I would prefer you stay here. This is an easier place to guard you. There is a single entrance and exit to this room. Once we assess the entirety of the situation, I'll have my team move you."

"I would like you to stay put a little longer, too, Miss Trollinger." Doc glanced at the monitors.

Katy, Doc's other nurse, walked into the room. "Quite the crowd." The woman was young and had a ton of moxie. "I've got the results of our patient's blood test, Doc." She handed over the folder to him. "Should everyone leave? I can escort them out. You know...for HIPAA regs?"

"They can stay." Cindy glanced around the room. "I have nothing to hide."

Could the woman tell that everyone was on the fence about whether to trust her or not?

Belle's heart went out to Cindy. She also knew what it was to feel alone.

Shane squeezed Belle's hand. She looked at him and saw concern.

"I'm fine," she mouthed, wondering how he could get into her head so easily.

"Katy, the patient has given her verbal consent. That covers the regs in my mind," Doc said. "Miss Trollinger, do you take sleeping pills?"

"Sleeping pills? No."

Doc's eyes narrowed. "You don't have a prescription for Ambien?"

"I don't."

"Strange, because this shows it's in your blood stream."

"Oh my God. How?"

"You had mentioned the last thing you remembered was stopping in Twin Falls on your drive to Destiny. The next thing you recalled was waking up on the floor of Lucy's, is that right?"

"Yes. It's all true."

Corey leaned forward. "Where did you stop?"

"At a diner there. I think it was called Donna's or Diana's. I can't remember. I got a cup of coffee."

"Did you talk to anyone?" Shane asked.

"Just the waitress."

"No one else?"

"Wait. There was this guy who was walking past my table and he spilled his drink all over me. He told me he was sorry."

Jason brought out a pad and began writing on it. "What did he look like?"

"Average looking. He did have a lot of tattoos. His accent seemed to be Russian."

Corey stiffened. "Are you certain?"

Everyone in Destiny had suffered from the Russian mob. Could there be a connection? It was well known that Kip Lunceford was working with Anton, the son of a dead kingpin in the criminal organization.

"I guess so, but why does that matter? The man had nothing to do with me passing out."

"He could've slipped something in your coffee without your knowledge, Miss Trollinger," Mr. Black said.

"But Ambien?" Shane shook his head. "That's an odd choice of drug. Rohypnol would've been more effective."

"That's true, but loss of memory is a rare side effect of Ambien," Doc informed.

"Oh my God. Are you saying that I might've been drugged?"

"It's a possibility."

Cindy looked so scared. Belle couldn't help but feel for her. "Why? Does this have anything to do with Kip Lunceford?"

"Miss Trollinger, I'll call the local authorities in Twin Falls and see what we can find out." Jason seemed to be coming around to believing the woman was telling the truth, though it seemed like the others were still on the fence. "Until we know for sure, you must remain here."

Cindy was trembling. "I sure could use a cigarette right now."

"You can't smoke in here," Katy snapped.

Doc held up his hand. "Relax, nurse. Cindy is our patient, not our prisoner." He turned to Black. "What if your agents escorted her to the side entrance to smoke?"

"That shouldn't be a problem at all."

"Perfect." Doc handed the blood test to Paris. "Miss Trollinger, I want to run a few more tests."

"Do you think that's necessary?"

"It's only a precaution to make sure everything is fine with you. For now, I want you to stay here. We will make it as comfortable as we can." He turned to Paris. "I'll talk with you out in the hall about the tests I want to run."

"Yes, sir." The tension between Paris and Doc was easy to see.

Cindy sighed. "May I ask for another favor?"

Easton nodded. "Of course."

"Find Kip. Put him away. If you can use me to get to him, I'm willing to do whatever you want." Tears welled in Cindy's eyes. "Just don't let him hurt anyone ever again."

Chapter Five

Belle took one more look at herself in the mirror. She wore her hair up. The sweater she'd chosen was a pale blue. "Not bad for a break-up date."

God, she hated what she had to do.

Shane would be arriving any minute to take her to the Thanksgiving dinner at the Dream Hotel. She still found it odd that Destonians still called the event "Dinner" since the meal actually started at nine in the morning with donuts and coffee from Lana's Bakery Palace on the town square.

Belle had learned the tradition had gotten started several years ago because of Gretchen and Ethel. The two women always went early to set up and to start cooking. One year, Ethel's two husbands, Patrick and Sam, had brought them donuts. The next year, more men and women showed up to help and to enjoy the breakfast fare. Year after year, it grew until the whole town came.

She and Amber hadn't enjoyed many Thanksgiving meals after their parents' deaths.

She'd been looking forward to the all-day event that went into the night, ending in a dance, for some time. Now, she dreaded it.

Ending it with Shane and Corey had to be done. It was the right thing to do. She wished the two handsome men could accept something casual, but both of them, especially Shane, seemed to want more from her.

She'd never been alone with Shane or Corey. They always came as a duo for all their dates—all three of them. But Corey was on guard duty for Cindy Trollinger with Jo Black until two.

Why am I so upset about breaking it off with Shane and Corey?
The truth was that they'd really only just gotten to know a little about
each other.

Because, like Amber says, I always lead with my heart.

Juan came into her bedroom. "Mom, Mr. Shane is here for you."

"Are you ready to go, young man?" She put her arms around her
boy and gave him a hug.

"Yes, ma'am. I also made sure all the other boys were ready, too.
Aunt Amber told me we'd be leaving in fifteen minutes."

She kissed him on the cheek. "You and the other boys line up at
the van and wait for her and your uncles."

"Can I talk to Mr. Shane first? Is that okay?"

She nodded, feeling a little ache in her heart. Juan cared about
Shane and Corey very much. Even though she would not be dating the
two brothers after today, she hoped they would still visit Juan and the
other boys. They were so good with them.

She and Juan walked out of the house and onto the porch. Shane
was tossing a football around with five of the orphans, who were
smiling ear to ear.

"Hey beautiful," Shane said, causing a round of giggles from the
boys. "Are you ready?"

"Yes, I am." *As much as I can be.*

"You look gorgeous."

She smiled, heading down the steps.

Amber's three husbands came out the side door.

"Boys, go get in the van." Emmett's firm tone was followed by a
warm smile.

Cody chimed in as Juan and the other orphans ran to the vehicle,
"You know we're going to have to get another twelve-passenger van
when the other boys arrive."

"I've been looking into getting us a bus," Bryant informed. "You
know our wife. We're going to outgrow these new buildings fast. I bet
we'll have fifty boys living here by the end of next year."

Emmett slapped him on the back. "That suits me fine."

Shane shook all three of the Stone brothers' hands. "Looks like you guys are on target for the fifteenth for the dormitory and barn to be finished."

Cody nodded. "Lucas is not only a great architect, but he's also quite the taskmaster with us and his crew."

"We're all set for the ceremony the Friday before Christmas, too, aren't we, Belle?" Bryant asked.

She smiled. "Yes, we are. You know Destiny. Any reason for a party."

Amber came out of the front door looking stunning. "We better get going or we'll all be late."

Shane came up to Belle and put his arm around her, making her warm all over. "Shall we?"

She nodded, reminding herself she had to do the right thing by him and by Corey.

* * * *

"This is your first Thanksgiving in Destiny." Shane squeezed Belle tight into his side, leading her to the truck. Whether she knew it yet or not, she belonged with him and Corey. "Get ready to have your socks knocked off, sweetheart. Corey and I are going to keep you on the dance floor all night."

"I'm sure you will. We have to save a seat for Corey for the big meal."

"For sure. He made me swear that I would do just that. We're all going to sit at the Blue family table."

"Shouldn't I be at my sister's table instead?"

"With all those boys, the Stone family table is quite full. Besides, Amber is the one who suggested we sit at my family's table."

"Sounds like her." Belle stopped in her tracks. "Shane, this isn't your truck. Whose is it?"

He'd decided to leave his brand new Ford 450 Platinum at home since it had bucket seats. "It's Dad Curtis's." Thankfully, his dad had agreed to let him take his completely restored baby, a 1976 Ford F100. The black beauty had a bench seat, so Belle could ride right next to him.

Her eyes were wide with amazement. "It looks almost brand new."

"Both my dads love to restore cars and trucks. It's a hobby that has actually paid off. They make almost as much money selling vehicles on the Internet as they do at Blue's Diner."

"Wow, I had no idea." She climbed into the cab, sitting in the middle just like he'd planned. "Is this one for sale, too?"

"Why? Are you in the market, sweetheart?" God, he was certainly ready to take Belle off the market.

She grinned. "Maybe."

"I'll talk to my dads and see if I can work something out for you." Even though Dad Curtis loved the truck, if Belle wanted it, he would find a way to convince his dad to sell it to her.

He started the engine and put his hand on her thigh. "I'm glad we get a moment alone, Belle. I need to talk to you about something." He needed her to understand why he and Corey wanted to keep her away from Cindy Trollinger.

"Can we talk after the meal, Shane? There's too much on my mind right now. Gretchen and Ethel assigned me to the team on stuffing. I've never made stuffing in my life."

"Sure. After is fine."

She sighed. "I have something I want to tell you, too."

He didn't like the sound of that one bit. "It can wait. Like you said. After the meal."

She smiled weakly.

Watching the little, subtle changes on her pretty face told him all he needed to know. She meant to break up with him today. With him and Corey. *Fuck.*

He squeezed her thigh. He wasn't about to lose her. They'd only begun dating, but he knew in his heart that she was the one for him. How she was with Juan and the other boys, hell, how she was with everyone floored him. She was kind and warm, loving and charming. He loved her sass and strength.

She leaned her head into his shoulder, and he could sense the turmoil underneath her surface.

Turning left onto The Narrows, he inhaled her scent of lilacs, or was it roses? Hell, he didn't know, he just knew she smelled terrific.

Whatever it took to make sure she remained right here next to him he would do.

Chapter Six

Belle looked around the packed banquet room of the Dream Hotel. After eating the donuts, everyone had worked very hard on the finishing touches of the big meal. Now, the crowd was enjoying all the delicious offerings.

"This dressing is amazing." Shane sat to her left, already on his second helping.

"You sure can pack it away." She was only halfway through her first plate and was already quite full.

Alice sat across the table from Belle, between her two husbands. "Both my boys are like their dads, sweetheart. They have quite the appetites."

"Yes, we do." Curtis leaned over and kissed her on the cheek. "Or were you talking about the food?"

Eddie laughed and put his arm around Alice. "Honey, you outdid yourself this year. This stuffing is the best ever."

"I had help. It wasn't all me."

"But you were the one in charge." Belle had been amazed at the coordination and bonding that had gone on between all the women in town making the meal. She'd never felt closer to a group of ladies than she did in Destiny.

Shane grabbed her hand. "Would you like some dessert, sweetheart?"

"I couldn't. Not for a while."

"How about we go for a drive? There's something I want to show you. When we come back, I bet you'll be ready for some." He squeezed her hand. "I can't wait to try a slice of your apple pie."

Looking into his gorgeous blue eyes, she felt her insides quake. A drive might be the perfect opportunity to do what she had to do, to tell him what she had to say, to end what should've been ended days ago.

"Maybe I should stay and help serve." *I'm not ready. Not yet. Just a few more hours are all I need.* But she knew no matter how long she delayed, it wouldn't make the moment any less difficult and sad.

"Honey, there's plenty of us to handle that." Alice's face lit up.

Belle imagined how wonderful it would be to have her as a mother-in-law. *But that can never be. I can never give her grandchildren. It wouldn't be right.*

"Belle, let our boy take you on a drive. If the ladies need help, Curtis and I can pitch in." Eddie winked. "We know a thing or two about kitchens. We do run the diner, you know."

"I surrender. I'll go on a drive with your son."

Shane stood and offered her his hand. "We won't be gone too long."

They walked to the pickup and he opened the door for her. He got in on the driver's side and pulled her in close to him. His arm remained around her shoulders. The feeling of his warm body next to hers gave her tingles.

How am I ever going to tell him that this is over? My heart is telling me "no" but my mind is telling me it is the right thing to do.

Shane turned the radio on low and a love song filled the cab. He leaned over and kissed her on the cheek.

Damn, he's making this hard.

She took a deep breath, trying to steady her nerves. Doing the right thing was proving to be more difficult than she'd imagined.

"I can't wait to see what you think about what I'm going to show you, Belle."

Glad for the distraction from her pending task, she turned to him. "Tell me what it is. Don't keep me in the dark."

He laughed. "Patience, baby. You'll see it soon enough."

Not wanting to remain quiet, knowing her mind would slip right back into mulling over having to break up with him and Corey, she decided to keep pushing for an answer. "Is it something everyone in Destiny has seen?"

As he drove up one of the mountains that surrounded Destiny, he grinned. "What is this? Twenty questions?"

"That's a great idea. Yes. Let's play twenty questions."

He grabbed her hand and squeezed. "That's one of your traits I love. Always moving forward, pushing for what you want. You've got such moxie and fire. You have me under your spell, that's for sure."

And you have me under yours, Mr. Shane Blue. "Good. You know how to play the game?"

"I do, but we're almost there, baby." He turned down a dirt road and came to a gate.

"Where are we?"

"This is my parents' land. Dads were raised on a ranch and wanted to make sure that Corey, Phoebe, and I grew up the same way. It's not a big piece of land but we are able to run a few head of cattle on it."

"This is what you wanted to show me?"

"Almost there, sweetheart." He jumped out of the truck. "You drive through when I open the gate."

"Good. I wanted to get behind the steering wheel of this baby."

Shane grinned. "I bet you did."

She slid into the driver's seat, adjusting it for her height so she could reach the pedals.

Shane walked over to the gate, putting the key in the lock that fastened the thick chains together. He swung it wide and motioned her to drive through.

When she was on the other side of the gate, she watched him in the rearview mirror, shutting and locking it. As he took a few steps to the truck, she hit the gas, moving about ten feet from him. He shook his head and started walking for the truck. She laughed and hit the gas again, keeping the distance. Then he ran, making it to the driver's side door.

She gave him her sweetest smile. "I told you I wanted to see what it was made of."

"Yes, you did." He put his hand on the back of her neck and pulled her in close, pressing his lips to hers.

She melted into him. *God, this isn't what I need to be doing, but damn, this cowboy knows how to kiss.*

"If you want to drive the truck, I'll let you take the wheel when we head back."

"You really would trust me after what I just did?"

"I probably shouldn't, but yes." He slid into the cab.

She scooted over just enough to give him room. "This is beautiful. How high up are we?"

"We're over a thousand feet above Destiny." He turned right and stopped the truck in a clearing, putting it in park. She saw the entire valley spread out below them. "This is what I wanted to show you, Belle."

"It's breathtaking." She could see the whole town. "It looks so small from here." She could make out O'Leary Global and TBK tower.

"This is my favorite spot in the world. Since I was a kid, I would come here and stare at the entire valley. It made me appreciate all that I had. My family. My friends. No matter how big my problems were, up here I knew they were small and that I could overcome them."

Her heart began to break. "Not all problems are fixable, Shane."

Belle felt too much for him. She wanted everything he was offering—a chance at moving things to the next level. If only she had a different body, one that wasn't damaged, one that could bring life into the world. But she didn't.

He pulled her in close. "I know you've been through so much, Belle. You and Amber were young when your parents died. That's got to be hard on anyone no matter how old they are, but as teenagers it must've been devastating. You've never given up. Don't start now."

Belle realized that Shane must've sensed what she meant to do today. "There's more about me than you know. It's just—"

He placed his finger to her lips. "Look how big these mountains are. They've been here long before any of us and they will be here long after. They don't worry. They just keep on. That's what you do. I've seen how you are with those boys, especially Juan. You're their angel, sweetheart, straight from heaven. The light that appears on those kids' faces whenever you are near is something to behold. Can't you see what you do to me? I'm a different man because of you, Belle. You know my story. Three years in the pen working undercover for the government. It changed me. I stopped believing in the goodness of most people. The only thing I clung to was my family, my town, my home. Everything else I pushed away. I didn't want more. My work became my only purpose. But you came into my life and changed me. I want more. I want a future. I want you."

"This is too fast, Shane." *I can't do this. I just can't.*

"I care about you, Belle, and I can tell you feel something for me, too." Shane pulled her in tight, locking his eyes on hers. "If you want to go slow, then I will go slow, but I just needed you to know how I feel."

"I don't want to go slow, Shane. I want to go fast. I want all of it, but—"

He silenced her with another kiss, this one deeper and more passionate. His tongue traced her lips and she sighed into him, loving the feel of his mouth on hers.

Shane tasted like the future, like hope, like the promise of something that could last. With every fiber of her being, she wanted that, wanted to remain by his and Corey's sides, wanted to dream the impossible. She'd tried to lead with her head but her heart had taken over.

She molded her body into his and he continued kissing her into a state of warmth. She felt him cup her breasts, massaging them so gently through the fabric of her top.

Her lips throbbed and her heart began to race. Panting, she felt her need expand inside her.

"Oh, Belle, I won't ever let you go." He slipped his hands inside her sweater and unfastened her bra.

As his manly lips moved to her shoulder, she felt her temperature rise. The pressure inside her grew and grew.

"I want you, baby. I want all of you."

God, help me, I'm leading with my heart.

She reached up, locking her hands around his neck. "I want you, too, Shane. More than anything, I want you."

This was the first time she was going to be intimate with him. She'd been dreaming about it for some time, ever since their first date. But it also must be the last time. She couldn't let herself fall even deeper than she already had.

One time. That's all.

No matter what, it was going to hurt like hell. Shane had shared his feelings for her. She knew it was going to hurt him, too, but better now than later. He deserved a woman who could give him children. He was going to make a wonderful dad one day.

Continuing to ravage her mouth, Shane removed her sweater and bra. His hands moved over her breasts, raising her desires to a maddening level, quieting her mind. His flesh touching her exposed skin increased the pressure growing in her body.

"Baby, your breasts are so soft and beautiful." He bent down and feathered his lips over her nipples, causing them to tingle and ache.

"Oh my God, I love your touches, Shane. You're making me burn." She unbuttoned his shirt and slid it off his shoulders. "You've got a beautiful chest, too, Mr. Blue."

He laughed. "Want to touch it? Be my guest, baby."

She grinned and ran her fingers over his muscled pecs, circling his nipples. Kissing, their hands roamed, discovering every inch of each other through touch. She felt a tingle spread from her belly throughout her body until her pussy began to dampen.

She panted, feeling lost to her thirst. "More."

"You took the word right out of my mouth, angel." Shane unfastened the button of her jeans. Slowly, he unzipped them. "God, your scent is so sweet."

When he slid his thick fingers under her thong, she arched into him. The throbbing of her lips, nipples, and clit seemed to join into a giant ball of desire as the pressure took her breath away.

Lost to her passions for him, she unbuttoned his Levi's and sent her hand inside, grabbing his thick cock. It was so massive. She couldn't bring her fingers around the shaft.

His eyes, laden with lust, locked in on her. "Yes, baby. God, that feels so good."

"I have the power, don't I?" She smiled, running her fingers up and down his shaft.

He grinned. "Hardly." He laid her back on the bench seat, slipping off her jeans and thong. When his fingers threaded through her wet folds, she gasped. "See. I'm in control here, baby. Always."

Even through her rapid heartbeats, she found the will to tilt her head to the side. "Really?" She began pumping his dick as fast as she could.

"Ah." His eyelids narrowed and his breathing deepened. "Angel and devil. I like." With one hand, he reached up and pinched her nipple. With the other, he pressed his thumb on her clit.

The pressure reached another level of insanity. "You win. Please. God." She released his cock.

"I always win, Belle." He slipped off his jeans and she saw how monstrous his cock was. At least ten inches of pure masculinity. "That's something you should know."

"I'm beginning to believe you."

He smiled wickedly and without a word shifted his tall frame in the cab until his mouth was hovering over her pussy. The hot gusts from his lips were driving her insane.

"Please, Shane. Stop teasing me. I can't stand much more."

"That's what I like to hear." He grabbed her thighs and he leaned forward.

When his tongue landed on her pussy, she pressed on the back of his head. Every one of his lusty licks spurred her faster, hotter, and higher. She was aroused and on fire, burning from the inside out.

He captured her clit between his lips and applied a dizzying pressure.

"Oh my God, Shane. Yes." The pressure inside exploded into a million shivering sensations.

"Yes, baby. Come for me." Moisture pooled out of her and he drank every drop.

He'd given her a climax like none other she'd ever felt before.

Crazed from the orgasm, she clawed at him. "Shane, I need more of you. God, I must have more."

"I want to be inside you, baby. I want to feel all of you." He moved his muscled frame up her body, pinning her to the seat.

Feeling the tip of his cock touching her pussy, she wrapped her legs around his waist.

"I can't stand it." She was shivering with need from head to toe. "Take me, Shane. Please."

Though she'd heard about multiple orgasms from other women, she'd never experienced them herself. Was it about to happen for her?

He kissed her again and sent his cock into her depths. The feel of him sent her over the edge once again. And then it happened. Her first multiple orgasm. She came again. Every nerve in her body sparked with heat.

"God, you are so tight, baby. Feels so good." His thrusts came fast and furious.

"Yes. Yes. Yes." She raked her fingernails over his shoulders, her desires building once again.

Shane, the sexy beast, claimed every inch of her body. He grabbed her wrists, holding them in place. Oddly, the restraint added to her heat and frenzy.

He thrust his cock deeper into her pussy.

Dizzy and burning, she writhed under him as another wave of pressure continued to build. The pounding in her chest seemed to mirror his every thrust. Each plunge of his cock invaded her completely, totally—reaching places that had never been touched before.

His breathing was labored as his chest rose and fell like a rumbling volcano. "Come for me, baby."

She came and came and came, trembling like mad. A flood of overwhelming sensations swamped her entire being. She screamed, something she'd never done before in sex, but she couldn't hold back. Not now. Not with him.

"Fuck. Yes. Ahhh." He came, shooting his seed inside her.

Her pussy clenched and unclenched and clenched again on his thick cock. Then a swarm of shivers overtook her. She writhed under him, unable to remain still.

He rained down soft kisses on her, holding her close.

"That was amazing, Shane."

He gazed at her with such loving eyes, melting her into a puddle. His jaw dropped. "Oh my God. I was so lost to the moment that I forgot to use protection. I'm sorry."

"I was lost to it, too. We acted like two teenagers, didn't we?" She grinned. "Don't worry, Shane. It'll be okay." Her heart began to rip in two. *There's no need for protection. I can't have his child.* She felt her eyes begin to well up with tears.

"We'll make sure it's okay. I know you said this was fast, but so what. If we made a baby today, it will be the happiest day of my life, Belle."

She choked back her tears, looking straight into Shane's eyes. *If only miracles happened, but they don't.*

Chapter Seven

Corey walked into the banquet hall of the Dream Hotel with Jo Brown.

They'd been on guard duty for Cindy Trollinger for the past eight hours. Now, Black and Jason were manning the post at her door. Shane was next up in the rotation and would be taking over for Black.

Jo smiled, which was unusual for her. She'd let her walls down a little over the past eight hours. They'd both talked about their childhood, and it turned out, Jo had an unusual one indeed.

Only a few years older than he, she was quite an attractive woman, though of late, he only had eyes for Belle.

"Looks like things are winding down, Corey."

"The main meal is done, but things are hardly over. You've never been to the Thanksgiving Bash in my hometown." He looked at his watch. "It goes way past midnight."

"The more time I spend in Destiny, the more I see why people love it here."

The tables were being cleared even though a few late arrivals, like him, were just sitting down to eat. There was no sign of either Belle or Shane anywhere.

Jo stifled a yawn. "I'm going to grab a plate and head back to my hotel room. I'm beat."

"Get some rest. I'll see you tomorrow back at our post."

She nodded and walked away.

Corey glanced around the room, looking for his parents or his sister. They might know where Belle and Shane were, but the rest of his family was missing as well. Made sense. Most had finished their

Thanksgiving meal hours ago. Likely, along with the bulk of the crowd, his family and Belle had moved into the other room at the hotel where the dance was being held.

Doc and Mick were at a table to his right.

"Have you seen my brother or Belle, fellas?"

Mick shook his head.

Doc looked up at him. "I saw them head out a couple of hours ago, Corey."

He didn't like the sound of that.

Shane had made it clear on more than one occasion that he was ready to get more serious with Belle.

Way too early for that.

"There they are." Mick pointed to the door.

Corey turned and saw the duo enter the hall. Shane's face was lit up like a Christmas tree. His brother's arm was around Belle, who had a completely different look than Shane. She looked somber.

Where have they been? What did they do? If he only went by what Shane looked like alone then there was no doubt what had happened.

He's had sex. But why did Belle look so serious? What was going through her mind?

I hope Shane didn't push her into something she wasn't ready for.

When her eyes locked on his, she smiled weakly and he felt his gut tighten.

"Hey, bro." Shane waved at him, smiling from ear to ear. They walked over to him. "How was your shift?"

"Uneventful." Corey grabbed Belle's hands. "Don't forget that you promised me and Juan and the other boys to join us tomorrow for Cody's next dragon hunting ride. That will be eventful for sure."

"How can I forget? You and the boys won't let me."

"It's because we're all crazy about you. How about a piece of apple pie, darlin'?"

She nodded. "I hope you like it. No promises."

Corey wanted to have a moment alone with Shane to get to the bottom of what had happened between him and Belle. Filling his plate was all the excuse he needed.

Shane grabbed her hand. "Have you eaten Mom's stuffing yet? It's scrumdiddlyumptious."

Corey fixed his hot stare on Shane. Was his brother aware of how Belle was feeling? Shane usually could sense so much in anyone. *Why is he not seeing how torn up Belle is?* "Where have you two been?"

"Shane took me to your parents' land." The light returned to her eyes. "It is so beautiful up there."

Corey decided to prod a little. He needed to uncover what was troubling her. "Did you have a good time?"

She nodded and smiled. "We did."

They definitely had sex. She seemed fine with that. So, what else could be troubling her?

"I've only got a half hour before I have to take Black's place at the clinic." Shane pulled out a chair for Belle. "Let me get us dessert. I want to have at least one dance with you before I have to leave."

She smiled. "I'd like that."

"We'll be back, beautiful." As they got out of her earshot, Corey turned to his brother. "What the hell is going on?"

Shane shrugged. "I don't know what you're talking about."

"You're the mind reader in our family. How can you be so blind? Belle is upset about something. It's as plain as day."

"I really don't want to go into it now, bro."

"Tough. Clearly you do know she's troubled by something. I know you had sex. What happened to upset her?"

"The sex was incredible. She and I were like teenagers. We both gave in to our desires and it was wonderful. Nothing like it has ever happened to me before." Shane turned to him, his face filled with reverence and gravity. "I care about Belle. I think she could be the one for us."

Trying to slow Shane down was going to take some effort, but he knew it had to be done. His brother wasn't ready to jump right into a serious relationship, no matter how wonderful Belle was. "That still doesn't explain why she is so unsettled."

Shane sighed. "I forgot to use protection because I was so lost in the moment. She said it didn't matter, not to worry. But her mood immediately took a turn from sunny to gloomy."

"Damn it, Shane. No wonder she's upset. What if she's pregnant? Then what?"

"I told her that it would make me the happiest man in the world, and I meant every word of it."

"You keep trying to push her into something permanent and it is obvious she's not ready for that."

"I'm not so sure, but I hope I haven't fucked it up." Shane got two plates and filled them with Belle's apple pie.

"I hope you're right. We just have to take things a lot slower with her."

"What about you, Corey? It's obvious that you are into Belle as much as I am. Why are you holding back?"

"Because like her, Shane, you are not ready for something serious." Corey could imagine one day, a few years down the road, planning a future together. Just not now.

Unless she's pregnant. That would change everything.

Though it would be like moving from a standstill into the fast lane, having a child with her would be amazing. Corey would love to be a father. Shane loved children just as much as he did and would be a great parent. What about Belle? Corey smiled. She'd already shown him what kind of mother she was going to be. The loving way she took care of Juan and the other boys at the Stone Ranch told him all he needed to know.

They walked back to Belle with the dessert.

He sat on one side of her and Shane sat on the other.

"Your apple pie looks delicious, sweetheart." Corey grabbed his fork.

She shook her head. "Shouldn't you start with the main meal first before moving on to dessert?"

"There's no rule that you can't have dessert first, at least not in Destiny." He took a bite of the pie. The crust and filling were perfection. "Oh my God, where did you learn to bake like this?"

She grinned. "From my mom. You really like it?"

"Corey never lies, baby." Shane took a bite of the piece on his plate. "Wow. This is good. Really good."

"I hope everyone that tried my pies enjoyed them as much as you two." The blue mood she'd come in with seemed to be lifting some.

"I'm sure they did, Belle." He took another bite. "We got the last three pieces."

"No kidding. That's great. Those girls from the high school worked hard. I'll have to let them know. I wonder where they are?"

"At the dance, no doubt." Shane's plate was empty. "I'm on a time crunch, sweetheart. I'd like my dance."

She laughed. "Corey, has he always been so pushy?"

"Only since we were kids." He put his arm around her shoulder. "I still say our parents spoiled him and Phoebe. I'm the sensible one of the three of us."

"I can see that." She sent him a sweet wink and then turned to Shane, offering her hand. "A promise is a promise."

They all stood and walked over to the room where the dance was going on. Wolfe Mayhem, Mitchell's band, ended one song and segued right into another, this one being a fast country song.

"You know the line dance that goes with this one?" Shane asked her as the crowd of boot scooters were lining up across the floor.

She nodded. "It's so much fun. Let's go."

Corey watched them laughing as they kicked and stepped in time with the rest of the dancers. It was good to see them having so much fun. He walked over to the bar and got a beer and a glass of wine for Belle, which he knew she preferred. Shane was going to be on guard duty so he got him a bottled water. He walked back with the drinks just as the band changed to a slow tune.

Shane held Belle close. The look on both their faces told Corey they were already falling hard for one another. As the song ended, Shane kissed her tenderly, and they walked over to him.

He handed them their drinks.

Belle smiled. "Thank you. You remembered I love red wine."

"Of course I did, sweetheart."

Shane looked at the time on his cell. "I've got to go." He leaned over and kissed Belle again. "I'll miss you."

"I'll miss you, too, but you're leaving me in good hands."

Corey liked the sound of that, though he could still sense some hesitation in Belle. No wonder, given what he'd learned from Shane. He would make it his job for the rest of the evening to make sure she had a good time.

"Take good care of our girl, bro."

"You know I will."

Shane left.

He put down his beer and grabbed her hand. "I want a dance with the most beautiful woman in Destiny."

Belle smiled and glanced around the room. "Where is she?"

"You know exactly where she is, sweetheart. She's right in front of me." He kissed her, relishing the taste of her lips.

Her face was flushed. "I'm not going to argue with you about the most beautiful, but I do suggest you go see an eye doctor." She laughed and ran to the middle of the dance floor. "What are you waiting for? I'm ready to dance, Mr. Blue."

Stepping up to her, he wrapped his arms around her. "Let's show them how it's done."

He spun her around the dance floor and loved how good she was on her toes. "You sure know how to move your pretty feet, darlin.'"

"And so do you, marshal."

They stayed out on the dance floor through a ton of songs, back to back. He hadn't had that much fun...*ever*. Belle's smile thrilled him.

He grabbed her hand. "You're out of breath. Let's take a break."

She nodded, and he led her to some chairs in a far corner.

"Would you like another drink, sweetheart?"

"I'm fine, but I wouldn't mind taking a drive, Corey. Back up to your parents' place."

"To the lookout? I'd be glad to, but why? Aren't you having a good time?"

"I am. I'm having a wonderful time, but I just would like to see it at night. I've got a lot on my mind and Shane told me how being there helped him get perspective over his troubles. Problems don't seem so big when you're looking at those mountains surrounding Destiny."

Problems? Was she still worried about not using protection?

"Sure. Let's go."

* * * *

Belle leaned her head against Corey's shoulder.

The sun had set and the outside temperature was quite chilly. He'd left his truck running and the heat on, so they were nice and toasty.

"I love it here. I can't imagine how wonderful it must've been growing up in Destiny." She gazed down at the town, which looked like little points of light that were also reflected on the lake's still surface.

"Shane, Phoebe, and I have wonderful childhood memories. What about you and Amber? You told me and Shane about losing your parents when you were in high school. I can't even imagine how hard that was. What was your childhood like?"

She loved how sweet Corey was being. "Our mom and dad were very loving. The best."

He kissed her hair. "I'm sure they would be proud of both their girls."

"I miss them very much." She locked her fingers over his hand. "It's hard for Amber, too. She was only a couple of years younger than me when they passed away. We've clung to each other ever since. I try to be there for my sister in every way I can, but it's not the same as it would've been had my parents lived."

"Baby, you were so young when you lost them. You can't beat yourself up. Anyone can see that you've been and continue to be a great sister to Amber."

"Thank you. You know, Corey, my mom would've loved being a grandmother." She closed her eyes, taking in a deep breath of regret. "I'm going to love being an aunt, that's for sure.

Corey touched her cheek. She opened her eyes, looking at the concern on his face.

"What's wrong, Belle? This isn't just about Amber's baby, is it?"

He was getting too close to the truth. *To my truth.* "I don't want to talk about that right now."

"Sure you can. I'm here. I want to help." His tender words were crushing her heart.

She needed to have more courage. It was wrong to keep leading him and Shane on when there could never be a future. They deserved to be fathers. No matter how much she wanted to stay, she couldn't take that away from them. Shane had made it clear to her that he wanted a serious relationship. Corey, of the two, seemed okay with something more casual. God, if only that was still possible. But she'd led with her heart and gotten in way too deep.

"Corey, this isn't going to work. You, me, and Shane. It's just not possible." The words came out and she instantly wished she could take them back. "I've said too much."

"No. You haven't said enough." His tone deepened.

She couldn't tell him. Not now. It wouldn't be fair to Shane. She needed to tell them both, face to face. "Tomorrow. I promise I'll tell you and Shane everything."

Seeing Corey's face darken surprised her. "We can talk tomorrow, Belle. But no matter what you have to say, trust me, what we have—you, me, and Shane—it's not over. Not even close. Not now. Not ever."

Taken aback by how forceful he was being, she blinked several times. "I thought you wanted something fun but casual. I must've misread your intentions."

"I was willing to keep it casual until right now. Let me show you my new intentions, baby." He crashed his mouth to hers, devouring her lips. He pulled her in close against his muscled body, and she melted into him, unable to resist.

I shouldn't do this.

"Does that tell you exactly what my intentions are, sweetheart?" He didn't wait for an answer, but kissed her again with such urgency it took her breath away.

She'd never seen him like this before, so dominant, so intense. Had her confession that she was ready to end it ignited something possessive inside him, something that wasn't willing to let her go? She knew it had.

He stripped her of her clothes so fast it made her head spin and her body burn.

It might be selfish of her, but she had to be with him—*at least once.*

She could feel his hunger on his every breath.

He ripped off his shirt, sending a few buttons to the floor of the truck. In a flash, he was out of his Levi's. His ten-inch cock was thick and firm.

"I have protection. Don't worry."

Her heart seized in her chest. "No."

A storm erupted on his face. "You don't want me?"

"Yes."

"Yes? No?" He cupped her chin. "Which is it?"

"I'm not making any sense, am I?"

"That's putting it mildly. Nod your head if you want to me to make love to you."

She nodded with all her might.

"That's all I need to know." He grinned, but it didn't soften the manly force he was exuding from every pore in his muscled body. "Let me get a condom out of my pocket."

He reached for his jeans and she grabbed his wrist. "No."

"Belle, you have to stop teasing me. Now."

"I'm not teasing you. I want you. I really do, but we don't need protection."

"I don't understand. Why?"

"Just make love to me now."

"Are you on the pill?"

"I am." The little white lie wouldn't hurt him. She wanted him so badly and couldn't bear even a condom coming between them. "Corey. I need you so much."

He kissed her, making her toes curl. "And I need you, too, Belle. Your body is so beautiful." His hands cupped her breasts, and her skin began to warm. He grabbed her and sat her on his lap, facing him.

She could feel the head of his cock pressing against her wet pussy. Her need amplified to a dizzying pressure. She felt his hands on her back, pulling her into him. As his dick thrust into her channel, she gasped as he filled her insides to the max.

"You like having my cock in your pussy, baby?"

"Very much," she confessed breathlessly. "Yes. So good." She rode his dick like a crazy woman, enjoying the spots it was scraping inside her body.

She leaned back and he grabbed her breasts, massaging her nipples with his thumb and forefinger until they were throbbing. Her pussy ached and the burn in her body sizzled higher and higher.

He reached down and pressed on her clit, delivering just the perfect amount of pressure.

"Yes. God. Yes." She moved up and down his cock, getting closer and closer to the climax she had to have.

Keeping his thumb on her clit, he reached around her and fingered her anus, sending her over the top and into sweet, mind-blowing release. Her body erupted with overwhelming sensations, vast and satisfying, hot and wet, intense and complete.

Corey's facial muscles tightened, but his eyes never left hers.

"Fuuuck." He thrust up into her, and she could feel him unload his seed into her body.

"That was amazing." She kissed his chest as her shivers began to settle down a little.

His breathing was heavy. A smile spread across his handsome face. "More to come, baby. Now that I've had you, I want more. And. I. Will. Have. More."

How did he know that I needed him to be strong and somewhat forceful? I really believe he needed that, too.

Chapter Eight

Compared to most of the assignments Shane had been given, guarding Cindy Trollinger was one of the easiest—*so far.* Aside from her smoke breaks and her insistence that her car be started every day to save the battery, there was little to do.

Jason, his shift partner, looked at his ROC. "I'll be glad when we can use these again. I wonder when the tech trio will have the new security up and running."

"When Dylan and Nicole show, we can ask them." Shane knew Dylan had gone to TBK after the big dinner today. "I'm sure he'll have a progress report for us."

Jason smiled. "He always does. Dylan's a friend, but he isn't someone I would want to be on opposing sides."

"Me either, buddy." It felt good to be back to normal with Jason. "But Dylan has softened a little bit since him and Cameron finally settled down with Erica."

"That's for sure. I even saw a smile cross Dylan's face over at your parents' diner last week when he was having breakfast with Erica."

"You're one to talk, Jason." Shane looked at his future brother-in-law. Jason and his brothers were going to marry Phoebe in the spring. "My sister has definitely corralled you, Lucas, and Mitchell."

"It's true, and I'm happier than I've ever been." Jason took a deep breath and looked him straight in the eyes. "She's the love of my life and my brothers', Shane. What about you? When are you and Corey going to settle down? Everyone in town has seen you two with Amber Stone's sister, Belle. Seems to me she might be about to corral you and Corey."

"You sound like Ethel and Gretchen, Jason Wolfe. I never thought of you as a matchmaker."

"I'm not. Play all you want, Shane Blue. Bed a hundred women if you like. But I can tell you that the love of the right woman, that special someone…there's nothing like it on earth. You're my friend, Shane. I only want you and Corey to be happy."

It was so good to be past all the bullshit his undercover assignment had forced on him and Jason. "I'm ready to settle down with Belle. She is the one, but something is holding her back. Corey, too, seems to be trying to hit the brakes."

"Don't let him. Trust your gut, Shane. Do what you have to do to make sure you have a future with Belle. Corey will come around. You'll see."

They heard footsteps coming down the hall and both of them placed their hands on their weapons as protocol demanded, though it was likely their replacements.

Corey appeared at the end of the hallway. He walked over to them.

"Your shift doesn't start until six in the morning, bro." Shane looked at the time on his cell. *9:51 p.m.* The dance wouldn't end for a couple more hours. "What are you doing here and where is Belle?"

"I just dropped her off at Stone Ranch. She was exhausted from all the cooking yesterday and today. Also, I came because I wanted to get an update on this Trollinger and Kip issue."

Something on Corey's face told him there was more to the story than just exhaustion and that he'd come for more than just wanting to be filled in on what was going on with their mission.

More footsteps. This time, the expected duo, Dylan and Nicole, walked up to them.

Dylan, in typical Dylan fashion, didn't wait for "hellos" or handshakes but jumped right in. "Good news, men. The tech trio believes they've come up with something to keep Lunceford out of our systems. Our ROCs will be fully functional and secure by ten tomorrow morning. Jena wants us all to log on ten minutes later. She and her guys will run a couple of tests. If all goes well, after that, we should be good to go."

Nicole turned to Shane and Jason. "How was the shift?"

"Quiet. Dead quiet." Jason always carried quite the load, being Swanson County's main peace officer. He cared deeply and took his job as sheriff very seriously. "Besides the ROCs, did Black or Jo dig up anything else on Lunceford or Trollinger?"

Nicole nodded. "I just saw Black at the dinner. The agents in Seattle found an envelope in the mailbox mentioned in the letter Kip sent to Cindy. Inside was five hundred thousand dollars' worth of diamonds. They've got to be some of the jewels Lunceford stole from Anton Mitrofanov's father back in Chicago."

"I'm beginning to think Cindy is telling the truth," Jason said.

Corey pointed to the closed door of Trollinger's room. "There's no way that Kip's sister isn't part of some bigger plan, whether she is telling the truth or not."

"Did they find anything else?" Shane looked at his teammates. The bond he felt with them and the other members was deepening.

Nicole continued, "A note addressed to Cindy. It was from Kip telling her to meet him in Aberdeen, which is about two hours from Seattle. The agents went there and discovered a warehouse full of computer equipment."

"What about Kip?"

She shook her head. "They believe he had been there though. The place looked just like the kind of command base Lunceford has set up before. There are agents in place in case he or any of his associates return. Our tech trio will get all the recovered equipment by tomorrow. You know them. They'll be able to use what they find in it to help us with our search. I think we're closing in on the asshole." Nicole's words were met with all of them nodding their heads in agreement.

"God, I hope so." Jason sighed.

"We also got a verification on Trollinger's story about the man bumping into her at Donna's Diner in Twin Falls," Dylan said. "A waitress remembered the incident and gave an accurate description of Cindy. She also said the guy who spilled the drink on her had tattoos down his arm and spoke with a Russian accent."

"Everything Trollinger has told us seems to be true." Corey was clearly beginning to come around some, if only some, that Cindy might be telling the truth about everything.

Shane wondered if he'd misplaced his distrust. Maybe the woman was in danger. Maybe Kip was really coming for her, though there'd been no sign of him coming to Destiny yet.

"Damn, that's some coincidence," Jason said. "Kip is known to be working with the Russian mob and it just so happens a man with tattoos down his arm is in the same diner with his sister."

"All we can do now is keep poking around in every hole we can find until we locate that damn snake," Dylan state flatly.

Jason nodded. "When it's quiet like this, we all know to expect the worst."

"Exactly why we must remain vigilant, sheriff." Dylan was one of the best agents in the entire CIA. "Flowers and I can take it from here."

"I'll be here at six sharp." Corey turned to Shane, his stare revealing he had more to say.

Shane patted Jason on the shoulder. "See you tomorrow."

Jason nodded and left.

He and Corey walked down the hallway to the back of the courthouse. "Did you park at home or here?"

"Truck is in the garage. Need to stretch my legs."

Just last week, he and Corey had rented a house on Second Street, one block behind the courthouse. Now that he didn't have parole to deal with, since his cover was no longer necessary, he didn't have to live with their parents. He and Corey were close, so residing together made sense.

Shane walked out into the brisk November air. Before crossing First Street, he turned to Corey. "So I know you didn't show up at Trollinger's room just to talk about the mission, did you?"

"No. You always can read me like an open book, can't you?"

"Yes, I can."

They crossed the street.

"Let's get home. Pour us a couple of drinks and then I can tell you what happened tonight. I just need to get my thoughts together. And make sure we are on the same page, bro."

Shane's gut tightened. "Belle is okay?"

"Yes, at least I think she is. But we do need to have a serious talk."

Five minutes later, they were in their house.

Shane grabbed a bottle of whiskey and poured drinks for him and Corey. They sat down at the kitchen table.

"Corey, what happened after I left the dinner?"

His brother filled him in, telling him about the drive back up to the lookout. "Belle is skittish, Shane. I could tell she was ready to bolt. I don't know what came over me, but I just couldn't let her go. We had sex, which blew my mind."

Shane nodded, recalling how incredible it had been to make love to Belle. "She's like no other, bro. I know."

"Belle kept telling me it would never work between the three of us but wouldn't say why. She told me she wants to talk to you and me tomorrow."

"Fuck. That doesn't sound good to me."

"To me either. I think the best course of action would be to see her separately for the time being. She may not realize that's best for her, but I'm sure it is."

"Not a bad idea. If we keep her from seeing us together, she won't have the chance to break things off with us."

"She's not from Destiny, so let her warm up to the idea of having two men. We can date her individually in the more traditional way— one on one." Corey took another gulp from his glass. "I know I told you to go slow. That's what I thought you needed, but now I know I was wrong. If we go too slowly we lose her. I'm sure about that."

"Me, too."

"I can't lose her, Shane." The intensity in his brother's voice shook him to his core.

He grabbed his shoulder. "We won't."

"She's holding back something. I can feel it."

"We have to work together to get her to open up. Once we know what she's dealing with, what is keeping her from committing to us, then we can turn things around."

"I can tell she cares for us. That's why I just don't get it. She keeps saying she wants to keep things casual, but I know that's a lie."

Shane nodded. "Whatever demons she's dealing with, it is past time for you and me to slay them."

"Damn right." Corey lifted his glass. "To our most important mission, Shane. To winning Belle's heart."

"Now that's a toast I can get behind." He clinked their glasses together. They both drank the rest of their whiskey.

"I better get some sleep. I've got to be back at Trollinger's room in the morning."

"Night." Shane watched Corey head to his bedroom. He poured himself another shot. It was good to have his brother by his side. They made quite the team.

Whatever it takes, you're ours, Belle. You'll see.

* * * *

For the millionth time that night, Belle glanced over at the blue numerals of her clock radio.

2:18 a.m.

No matter how tired her body was, her mind wasn't going to shut down and let her doze off.

She turned on her lamp. She'd already finished the book on her nightstand. It was a spicy tale by Sophie Oak, one of Amber's favorite authors.

Belle considered giving it a reread, but quickly decided against it. The tale was definitely worth it. But since every hot paragraph would only remind her of Shane and Corey, she knew cracking its pages would only add to her restlessness and already keyed-up body.

She clicked on the television. Nothing but infomercials. Whatever the two women on the screen were selling, she had no clue. Her thoughts were on Shane and Corey and nothing else.

Swinging her legs off the bed, she put on her robe. Time to see if a glass of wine might help with her current state of insomnia.

She walked out the door quietly, hoping not to disturb the rest of the people in the Stone house. A light was on in the kitchen. Someone else was up.

She tiptoed ahead and saw it was her sister standing at the kitchen sink. "What are you doing up so late?"

"Heartburn." Amber held up a glass of milk. "Thought this might help. Doc tells me it's normal at this stage of pregnancy."

Belle laughed. "Remember when Mom told us that when you have heartburn your baby is supposed to have a lot of hair."

Amber smiled. "Then I must be carrying Rapunzel. By the way, Sis, why are you up at this hour?"

"My heartburn is emotional, so I thought I'd have a glass of wine to settle mine down."

"Okay, since neither of us can sleep, why don't we sit down and talk."

"I'd like that very much." Belle filled her glass with her favorite merlot.

They sat down at the table together.

Amber took a sip of her milk. "Ah. That's better."

Belle brought her glass to her lips. The red liquid warmed her up quite nicely. "Yes, it is."

"So what mental issues are you dealing with? Is it still about Shane and Corey?"

She nodded. "Amber, I did just the opposite of what I should've done. I led with my heart and made a mess of everything."

"So you've completely fallen for them, right?"

"That's really an understatement." She took another sip of wine. Sleep wasn't going to happen tonight. "I'm in love with them, Sis. I can tell they have strong feelings for me. You should've seen them up at lookout point."

Amber smiled. "You went with them together?"

She shook her head. "No. Shane took me there first. It's on their parents' land, not far from here. It's beautiful. You can see the entire valley and town. It's a special place for both of them."

"You're stalling, Belle. Spill it."

"You know me too well, don't you?" She told Amber what had happened with Shane and Corey.

"Oh my God, Sis. This is wonderful news."

"You forgot, Amber, I can't have children. I shouldn't have let it go this far, but I needed them. I wanted to be held." She felt the tears well up in her eyes. "I'm just a selfish bitch."

"Stop it." Her sister grabbed her hand. "You deserve happiness."

She shook her head. "I can't let this go on. They are wonderful men and will make amazing fathers. I can't deny them a full life. It wouldn't be right."

"It's not right for you to choose for them. They deserve to know why."

"I know they do, Amber, but you should've seen their faces tonight. They both are ready to move things to the next level. In fact, Corey told me he wouldn't let me go ever. If I tell them I can't have children, I'm sure they will tell me it doesn't matter. They're such good men." Her voice began to shake. "I want them. I do. Maybe we could have several years together that would be amazing. But in five or ten years, I would look at them and know I had stolen something so special from them. I can't be with Shane and Corey. Can't you see that? It will break my heart, but I must push them away. I've come to terms with my illness and that I will never have my own child. That's my hell. I can't drag them down with me."

"Belle, you have not come to terms with anything. That's why you're still awake tonight. You want to be a mother. With all my heart, I want that for you. But even if you can't carry a child, it doesn't mean you aren't a mother. Juan is yours. You're his mother in every way. Doesn't he deserve to have a full life, too?"

"Yes, but I don't know what that—"

Amber held up her hand. "I just want you to wait before you make a final decision. Shane and Corey care about Juan, too. They're up here two and three times a week taking him horseback riding and dragon hunting."

"I know. Corey asked me to go on Cody's next dragon hunting ride with him, Juan, and the other boys."

"The four of you would make a wonderful family, Belle."

That image only broke her heart even more. "It just can't be."

"Just think about it. Okay?" Amber was quite persuasive.

"I love you, Sis, but what difference will waiting to think more on the issue make? That's all I've been doing since our very first date. Thinking. Over and over. I should've never agreed to go out with them in the first place. Now that I've slept with them it only makes things worse."

"Belle, I know you think breaking up is your only choice but you're wrong."

"I wish you were right, but I have to do this. Every second that passes I fall deeper and deeper in love with them. If my heart is to survive, I must end it now."

Amber squeezed her hand. "If you can't wait, then at least tell them the reason. Let them know why you believe you're not right for them."

"You're the only one that knows my truth, Sis." *Knows I'm a flawed woman.* "You're right. They deserve to know. I will tell them."

"I bet they will surprise you by what they say."

She shook her head. "I can't let that change my mind, Amber. I know you want it to, but I just can't. I hate this, but I know it's the right thing to do. The only thing to do. I'm going to fix this. I'm going to lead with my head this time." Belle's heart seized in her chest, reminding her of the hold it had on her. *I have to talk to them together. It's the right thing to do.*

Chapter Nine

The Boys Ranch Grand Opening was in one day.

It had been two weeks since Belle's late night talk with Amber. Funny, since they normally had their heart-to-heart sister talks in the early morning, but not so funny was that she hadn't been able to talk to the guys together.

Shane and Corey were on guard duty for Cindy Trollinger, but worked different shifts, making things impossible for Belle.

She'd made up her mind that she had to talk to them together. How long would Cindy be in town? How long before Lunceford was captured? She hoped soon, for the town and for herself. Avoiding Shane and Corey was becoming more and more difficult.

Coming to their parents' diner was a risk, as she might run into one of them, but she had an appointment with Alice, Eddie, and Curtis about the festivities.

Twelve new arrivals had joined Juan and the other boys. Things were crazy. They'd just learned this morning that two of the new boys had food allergies. She needed to make sure that their meals for the ceremony would be peanut free. The Blues were graciously providing all the food.

She walked into their diner.

Shane sat at the counter with Jason and Dylan. All their backs were to her, thank God. Shane hadn't spotted her.

I knew this was going to happen. I can come back later for the meeting.

She was about to back out the door and leave, when Desirae, one of the waitresses, handed her a menu. "Hey, Belle. Haven't seen you in here in a while."

Shane turned around and his eyes locked in on hers.

No, Desirae, you haven't because I've been avoiding facing Shane and Corey alone. "I'm not here to eat. I'm meeting Alice, Eddie, and Curtis about the Boys Ranch Opening."

"They're due in any minute. I think Alice is having difficulty getting Eddie and Curtis to leave their garage."

Shane's hot gaze never left her, making her squirm.

Desirae continued, "Did you hear about the 1970 Plymouth Barracuda they restored?

Despite her best effort, Belle hadn't succeeded in getting Shane and Corey together so she could break things off with them. Even though Amber had recommended she lead with her heart, Belle understood that being in a serious relationship with them wouldn't work, couldn't work.

"Belle, they got an offer from a rich dude in Australia. Can you believe it? Australia."

Belle watched Shane excuse himself from Jason and Dylan and head her way.

"The guy offered them a ton of money, but they aren't ready to part with it."

Shane stepped in front of her and Desirae, though his eyes remained only on her. "I can't blame my dads, Desirae, can you? It's their passion. They should keep the ones they love. Nothing should get in the way of passion."

Belle felt her knees weaken. He obviously wasn't just talking about his dads' love of classic cars.

Desirae smiled. "If you two want the booth by the window, it's yours."

"We'll take it." Shane was clearly done with the runaround she'd been giving him and Corey.

"I'm here to talk to your mom and dads, Shane. I can't stay long. I've got to head back to help Amber with all the planning."

I can't tell him alone. It wouldn't be fair to Corey. She must tell them together.

"My parents aren't here, Belle. You will have a cup of coffee with me." He grabbed her hand, and she felt something deep inside her respond to his demand.

"Fine. One cup." Anxiety grabbed hold of her.

They sat down in the booth and, instead of sitting opposite her, Shane sat right next to her. The heat of his muscled body radiated into her like a roaring fire.

"Shane, when your mom and dads show, I must talk to them. I really am busy."

His face stormed with frustration and anger. "You need to talk to me first, Belle. Why have you refused to go out with either Corey or me? You can't tell me things weren't going well between us."

"It's not that." *They were going too well.* "You both are so busy with protecting Lunceford's sister. I don't want to get in the way of that."

"Don't try to bullshit me. I've asked you to lunch several times. Corey has asked you to dinner. Each time, your answer has been no. What's really going on?"

She took a deep breath. "I need to talk to you both together, Shane. Not alone. Not one at a time. Together."

His eyes narrowed. "Why together?"

"Please, Shane." Her heart was breaking. "Not here. Not without Corey."

Alice came out from the back. "Belle, I'm so sorry for being late."

Shane shook his head. "Mom, your timing couldn't be worse."

"What's the matter, Son?"

"You're wrong, Shane. Her timing couldn't be better." Belle sighed. "If you'll let me out, I need to talk to your parents."

He slipped out of the booth, standing by his mother. "Tomorrow we talk."

"That's the Boys Ranch opening, Shane."

"Right. Okay, but we are not done, Belle." He walked away without another word.

She was quaking inside. She'd dodged a bullet, but how many more times would she be so lucky?

"Belle, I didn't mean to interrupt. We can talk later." Alice loved her children very much. The woman was an amazing mother.

"I don't have time, Alice." *No time at all.* "I must get back to the ranch as soon as possible."

She told her about the two boys who needed the special meals.

"No problem, Belle. We didn't use peanuts in anything. Everything is going to be just fine."

If only that were true, but I know better.

* * * *

Shane stood by the new bus that the Stones had purchased for the Boys Ranch. The all-day event was just now getting underway.

All the boys stood in front of the new dormitory that Lucas Wolfe had designed getting their picture taken. Juan was in the middle of the group. All the little cowboys were wearing the Boys Ranch uniform of Stetson hats, plaid shirts of various colors, Levi's, boots and specially made leather belts sporting buckles with the Stone's brand and their individual names.

The entire town had showed up for the grand opening to welcome the young men. It was clear by the smiles on the boys' faces and the looks in their eyes they felt important and accepted.

Belle held the microphone to introduce each boy. She looked stunning, as always. He loved the way her jeans fit her so perfectly.

She had her arm around Juan and was leaning down talking to one of the new boys who looked to be about five. She was wonderful with children.

"Ladies and gentlemen, I would like to present to you our newest residents to the Boys Ranch and to Destiny." Belle put her arm around the littlest of the boys, who had coal black hair and big brown eyes. She got down to his level. "This is Jake. Can you tell them how old you are?"

He held up his hand, spreading out his fingers. "This many."

"That's right. You are five years old."

The crowd applauded.

Jake smiled broadly. "I like my hat and boots, Miss Belle. Does that mean I'm a real cowboy now?"

Cheers shot up from everyone.

Belle kissed him on the cheek. "Yes it does, Jake. You are a real cowboy for sure."

Shane wasn't about to lose the most wonderful woman he'd ever met. She was everything he'd dreamed of and more.

She's mine.

Late last night, he'd told Corey about what she'd said to him at the diner yesterday. Despite their plan, Belle had been sidestepping their requests for one on one dates because she was determined to talk to them together. They had to devise a new plan.

Dylan and Easton walked over to him.

His boss held out his hand. "Nice party, Blue, don't you think?"

Shane took it. "It is."

"Your lady has put on quite a show for the town."

"Belle has been so busy getting this event off the ground we haven't had any time together. She's already helping with the O'Learys Christmas party planning. Hey, Dylan. I bet you and Cameron are excited to see Celeste and Caitlin. I heard they are going to be there."

"They are. My sisters can be a handful." A rare smile spread across the superagent's face. "The whole family is looking forward to their arrival. They didn't make it to the wedding, so Erica is excited to see them, too. Mom and Dads are ecstatic."

I've never heard Dylan talk so much in my life. The guy was usually quite precise and to the point. Married life was having a positive impact on him.

Shane turned his attention back to Belle, who stood next to Juan. "And of course, this last young man you already know." She handed him the microphone, pride showing on her face.

Shane felt it, too. He cared for Juan deeply.

"Thank you, Mom." Juan stood up straight. "It's my pleasure to introduce the founders of Destiny's Boys Ranch—Amber, Emmett, Bryant, and Cody Stone."

More applause erupted from those gathered around as the Stones moved to center stage.

Emmett took the microphone from Juan. "Let's have another round of applause for this young man, our very first resident of the Boys Ranch."

Shane couldn't help but smile for the boy who had won his heart.

"Before our young cowboys take you on tours of our new dormitory and barn, we would like to thank all of you for coming today to welcome these young men to our community. This was my sweet wife's dream and now it is a reality. We're going to teach these boys everything we know about ranching. Our boys will also be working with Kaylyn Anderson, learning how to train guide dogs."

Kaylyn came up followed by Jaris and Chance with their two guide dogs, Sugar and Annie.

Shane respected Jaris, as did everyone in Destiny. The man had taken a bullet for Nicole and had lost his sight. Chance, an African-American, had been blind since birth. He'd been coming to Destiny for years, getting dogs from Kaylyn for his students. Now both men were going to be living here and working with her.

Kaylyn definitely had eyes for Chance, as everyone in town knew. But today, it looked like she also had eyes for Jaris. Was something brewing between those three? "We're going to be giving a demonstration with the help of some of these fine boys over by the new bus."

"Thank you, Kaylyn." Emmett put his arm around Amber. "Our

goal is to not just turn these kids into cowboys but to see them grow into good men. Did I forget anything, baby?"

Amber smiled. "We've set up picnic tables out back for lunch, which is being provided by…"

As the Stones continued giving instructions about how the day was going to unfold, Shane turned to Black and Dylan. "Thanks for meeting me here."

"Not a problem," Black said. "Nothing new to report unfortunately."

Communication between the team was difficult, since their ROC devices were still offline. Jena, Sean, and Matt were still working on securing Shannon Elite's systems from Lunceford. They were getting closer but so far hadn't nailed it down.

"Our tech trio is fairly certain that Lunceford is in the Northwest. They identified another Lunceford command center from the equipment that was retrieved from Aberdeen."

"Where?" he asked.

"Montana this time, but still no Kip. The leads we've gotten from Cindy's letter have been the best to date. I'm not sure where we'd be without her."

The whole team seemed to be on board with Cindy now, believing her innocence. He remained a bit uneasy about Lunceford's sister, though everything about her story seemed to check out.

"It's been two weeks now since Trollinger came to town." The frustration in his boss's voice mirrored his own. "Something has to break soon."

"I need to ask a favor, sir. Corey and I need to be on the same shift."

Although they had planned on seeing Belle separately to keep her from bolting, it was time for him and Corey to change tactics.

"Done. I'll make sure that happens. Give me a day or two to work out the logistics."

"Thank you, boss." If Belle refused to see him and Corey

individually, then so be it. She was about to come face to face with them together, like she'd asked.

He grinned. *She's going to be surprised by what is going to happen.*

* * * *

"It's ten." Corey looked over at Jo. "Time to log into our ROCs." So far, none of the earlier tests had succeeded. Lunceford might be a psychopath but he was also quite brilliant.

She nodded and began running through the security hurdles on the device.

When he finished, his ROC opened up to a screen with a message from Jena telling them how the test would be conducted. It only took a few minutes, and another message popped up from her saying the test was a success.

"They did it, Jo."

She turned to him. "Lunceford shouldn't be able to get through the new security measures, but if he does, he won't get anything useful. This is quite impressive."

"Our tech trio is definitely up to whatever that fucker throws at us."

"I agree. The failsafe Jena built is pure genius."

"Yes, it is." If Lunceford or anyone somehow found a way to crack the new code, Jena's safeguard would warn the ROC's user by causing a red light to flash on the screen. Black's instructions were clear what to do when that happened. The agent was to shut down all communications and digital files immediately and report back to HQ.

After the test was done, Belle walked up to them carrying a box of donuts from Lana's Bakery Palace. "Thought you two bodyguards might be hungry."

Jo smiled. "After yesterday's meal at the grand opening, I shouldn't eat for a week."

"Me either, but you know we will." Belle handed Corey the box.

"Let me get us some coffee to go with these donuts, Corey. I could use a break to stretch my legs."

He knew Jo was only giving him and Belle a chance to talk privately. "Coffee would be good."

"How about you, Belle?"

"No thanks. I'm going to check on Paris's patient and then I've got to run some errands for the Boys Ranch."

"I'll be back shortly." Jo headed down the hallway.

He placed the box on his chair and pulled Belle in close. "I'm glad you're here, sweetheart. I've missed you."

She smiled. "I have missed you, too. I've been busy, you know."

Smile or not, he could see by her demeanor something was still troubling her. He and Shane knew what they had to do. Once Black rearranged the shifts, they were ready to do it.

He bent down and kissed her. She melted into him just like she was supposed to.

You are mine, Belle. I will make sure you know that.

He pressed his tongue against her lips, demanding entrance. She parted them and he devoured her.

He felt her delicate hands come up to his chest. She pushed gently against him.

Reluctantly, he released her sweet mouth. "Thank you for the donuts, baby."

"When can I talk to you and Shane together?" Her lips trembled, crushing him.

"I'm done at two and Shane takes the next shift."

She nodded. "If I come at two, maybe we can go to the side and let the other bodyguard handle things until I tell you what I need to tell you."

"That won't work." No way was he letting her take the reins. "Did you forget about Cody's dragon hunting ride with Juan and the other boys today? You promised. We can't let them down."

She sighed. "You're right. We can't. When does Shane's shift end?"

"Ten tonight."

"What about we grab a late meal at the diner. It should be pretty empty and we can talk."

Corey knew exactly what she meant to talk about. She was ready to break things off with him and Shane for good.

Whatever pain Belle was dealing with had to be killing her. He wanted to lift her burden and lighten her load. She deserved his very best, and he swore that was exactly what he would give her.

We are not over, Belle. You'll see. We will never be over. I love you, baby, and I know you love me, too.

"Dinner is a great idea, but not at the diner. I'll cook for us."

She shook her head. "That's too much trouble, Corey. You've been here since six and you and I will be helping Cody on the dragon hunting ride with the boys this afternoon. You'll be too tired to cook."

He gave her his best don't-question-me stare. "Dinner at mine and Shane's house." *That way Shane and I can be in control, not you.* He knew that was what she needed more than anything.

"There's no point in arguing with you, is there?"

"Sweetheart, now you're learning."

He touched her cheek.

She smiled.

God, you are so beautiful.

"Fine. Dinner at your house at ten. I'll be there."

"Why don't I just bring you after the hunting expedition, baby? We'll already be together."

She shook her head. "I'm going to have to clean up after riding with you and the boys."

"Okay, sweetheart. Bring an appetite."

She looked up at him and came to her toes. Then she kissed him, increasing his need to hold her, to have her, to possess her.

"Corey, I'm going to check on the patient."

She went into Trollinger's room.

He and Shane had agreed that Belle needed to open up to them, to be honest about what was really holding her back. Tonight, they would make sure she did.

* * * *

"How did you sleep?" Belle put the blood pressure cuff around Cindy's arm.

"I had things on my mind that kept me awake."

She knew the feeling. "Anything I can help you with. Is it about your brother?"

Cindy shook her head. "I try not to think about him. Besides, I've got all these wonderful people protecting me. I was just plagued about something that happened to me recently."

Belle couldn't imagine how difficult it was for Cindy, knowing she was related to such a monster. Having Amber as a sister was the exact opposite.

Amber is my rock.

"Your blood pressure is fine. If you'd like, we can talk."

"That would be nice. It's very lonely in here, you know." Cindy's eyes were welling up. "I'm grateful for having bodyguards, but they all look at me as if I'm the criminal instead of my brother." She turned her head away, hiding her eyes. "I've said too much. I'm sorry, Belle. This is just so hard."

She still had that odd feeling that there was more to Cindy than she was sharing. But was that her heart or her head talking? She was so mixed up with everything that was going on with Corey and Shane that she wasn't sure.

Wouldn't talking with Cindy help clear up any doubt about the woman's story? If there was more to learn, now was as good a time as any to discover it. Destiny was Belle's home now. If she could find out anything that might bring the town's most wanted monster to justice, she wanted to try.

"Cindy, I've been told I'm a good listener."

"You're a wonderful person, Belle." Cindy grabbed her hands and squeezed. A single tear fell from one of her eyes. "I lost a child a few months ago. A miscarriage."

Belle couldn't imagine what it would feel like to lose a baby. With all her heart, she felt for the woman. "I'm so sorry."

"Thank you. I wanted the baby more than you can imagine. The father isn't in the picture and I knew it would be difficult raising a child on my own. But I wanted to. Can you understand that?"

She nodded, feeling her own eyes well up with tears of regret.

"But now I think it might've been for the best, Belle. Kip Lunceford is my brother. We have the same genes. What if my child turned out to be like that monster?" Cindy's voice shook. "I've always wanted children. My whole life. I just wanted to be a mother. It might be old fashioned, but it's true. Now, I'm afraid to bring a baby into the world. I'm thinking about talking to Doctor Ryder about tying my tubes."

"Cindy, don't do anything permanent. I don't think there's anything genetic with Kip. I just think he's a selfish, mean bastard. I'm sure the prison system has run tests on him. I doubt there is anything you need to worry about."

"I hope you're right, but I just don't know what to think anymore, Belle."

"Having a baby is the most wonderful, rewarding feeling a woman can have. Back in Chicago, I worked in a maternity ward for several years. I've seen that special bond that only comes when a mother holds her baby for the first time. It's the closest thing to the divine that exists on earth. No words can express what a woman feels when she carries life inside her for nine months. She's the conduit to the world for her baby. Even after the birth, a mother never ceases to feel that magical connection. I'm so sorry you lost your baby. But there is time for you to have children, many, if you want."

"How many children do you have?"

Paris walked in, saving her from sharing her horrible truth with Cindy.

* * * *

Corey threw another log on the campfire he and the boys had built.

Off to his left, Cody had a group of three of the young hunters looking at rocks, though according to Cody they were clearly dragon fossils.

To Corey's right, Belle was keeping the rest of the young dragon hunters in line perfectly.

They were gobbling up their hotdogs and chips as fast as they could, anxious to get some last minute hunting in before they had to head back to the Boys Ranch.

All Belle needed to do was give them a stern look and they would settle down. A smile from her, and they would do anything she asked.

He couldn't get over how wonderful Belle was with Juan and the other orphans. Raising a family with her and Shane would be wonderful. Though Belle had never said she wanted to adopt Juan, Corey and Shane were pretty sure she did. That suited both of them just fine since they already felt a fatherly attachment to the boy.

Little Jake came up to Corey, his big brown eyes wide. "May I give the horses some carrots? Miss Belle brought some but told me I had to ask you first. My horse is hungry from all the dragon hunting."

He rustled the kid's hair. "Sure, but take Juan with you."

"Yes, sir." Grinning from ear to ear, Jake ran off to get Juan.

"I've got your plate ready, Corey." Belle waved him over to the blanket she'd spread out for the meal.

The boys were already done and off checking out the perimeter of the site for any signs of dragon tracks, their pockets full of cookies.

Even after riding for an hour, Belle looked as beautiful as could be.

"We'll head back in about fifteen minutes, sweetheart. That'll put us back at dusk."

She smiled, handing him a plate. "The boys had such fun today."

"Cody knows how to mesmerize them almost as well as Patrick O'Leary."

"He does sound like a true believer, doesn't he?"

"Of course he does, Belle. We're Destonians. We all believe in dragons." He put his arm around her shoulder and pointed to the three highest peaks across the valley. "When I was about Juan's age, I swear I saw a dragon circling right there."

"Now, you're just teasing me." She laughed. "Is it everyone's duty in town to make sure the unbelievers come into the fold?"

"Not officially, but we do win prizes when we convince someone. Are you becoming a believer yet? If you swear fealty to the dragons, I'll get a new grill for my house."

"So you're just using me, Mr. Blue." Her eyes sparkled. "Is that it?"

God, he couldn't get enough of her. "You caught me."

"Not hard to do, Corey. You're like an open book."

It was good to be out here with her by his side. She seemed more relaxed than she'd been in some time, but it was still obvious to him that her plan at dinner tonight was to end things with him and Shane. Not happening.

He'd talked with his brother about how they were going to get her to open up. Dinner. Wine. And then they would turn the conversation to why she was holding back. Once they knew her fears, then they would be able to win her for all time. That was the goal and that was exactly what was going to happen.

Jake screamed.

Instantly, they ran, reaching Jake just steps before Cody and the other boys.

Juan was on the ground, holding his hand. Corey and Belle got down on their knees next to him.

"I'm so sorry, Juan." Tears streamed down Jake's cheeks.

"It's okay." Juan looked up at Belle and held up his hand, which had two little wounds. "Rattlesnake got me, Mom. It was in a hollow log. Jake stuck his hand in. He thought it was a baby dragon. I pulled him away but the snake got me."

"He saved me," Jake choked out.

Juan's hand and arm were already swelling up.

Corey brought out his phone and called Doc Ryder. He put it on speaker.

Jake's eyes widened. "Is he going to die?"

"No, Jake." Belle turned to Cody. "Bring me my saddle bag."

Cody ran to her horse and brought back the bag.

"Hello." Doc's voice came through loud and clear, thank God. Reception up here was hit-and-miss most of the time.

"Doc, Juan got bit by a rattlesnake." Belle cleaned the wound on Juan's arm. "I've got everything in the kit you gave me."

"Give him the shot and keep the epinephrine ready."

"Sweetheart, relax." She stuck the needle close to the bite. "Everything is going to be fine."

The bars on Corey's cell went down and static came through, muffling Doc's voice. "You're doing great, Belle. Be sure… keep the epinephrine…in case you need it. Paris and I…set up here."

The line went dead. *Fuck.*

Cody had the boys standing back, and he was kneeling by the hollow log where the snake had been sleeping. "I sent a text to Emmett. He's driving to the crossing point to meet you. That way you can drive the rest of the way into town."

Belled kissed Juan on the cheek. "Sweetheart, relax. Everything is going to be fine."

Juan smiled weakly. He was being so brave. "I think I can ride, Mom."

She shook her head. "You need to stay as still as you can, baby." She turned to Corey. "You'll have to carry him."

He nodded. Corey was amazed at Belle's skill and how calm she was being. She knew what had to be done. She must've been pushing her fear way down deep.

"It's odd this time of year for a snake to bite, but it does happen sometimes." Cody retrieved the rattlesnake and cut off its head. "Bring this back with you to Doc Ryder. I'll take care of the rest of the boys. You two go. Get Juan to town."

Juan's breathing became somewhat labored.

Corey bent down.

"I'm going to cut your shirt off of you now, honey." Belle brought out some scissors from her bag. "Your arm is swelling and we don't want it to cause any constriction."

When she was done, Corey lifted the little dragon hunter into his arms, heading to the horses. "I love you, buddy. Just hang on. You're in good hands."

Chapter Ten

Several hours had passed since that damn rattler had bitten Belle's sweet boy. Juan's hand and arm had nearly doubled in size by the time they'd arrived. Her nurse's training had kicked in the very instant she'd heard little Jake scream even though she was terrified for Juan.

Belle watched Paris check Juan's IV drip. This was the hardest thing she'd ever faced in her life. Thank God, she didn't have to do it alone.

Amber was in the chair reading a magazine. Her sister had driven down with them in the Boys Ranch van. Amber's support meant the world to her.

Belle glanced over at Corey, who hadn't left her and Juan's sides.

He turned to her. "Our little guy has finally fallen asleep."

Corey had been so amazing with Juan, holding him in his arms while riding down the mountain on his horse. She'd followed, making sure to keep smiling in case Juan glanced at her.

Shane came into the room for the umpteenth time. "How's he doing?"

She smiled. "He's resting. Black is going to fire you if you keep leaving your station, Agent Blue."

Shane came over and put his arm around her. "I don't think so. Jason's got it covered. I'm allowed breaks. Besides, this little hero is more important to me than anything else at the moment."

He's right. Juan is a hero.

Juan had saved Jake. She hated seeing him like this, but knew he was getting the best care available. Plus, the entire town was in the courtroom, which was doubling as a waiting room at the moment, lending their prayers and support.

Paris grabbed her hand and squeezed. "He's doing great, Belle. Doc should be in any minute to talk to you."

Belle was glad to have such a good friend. "I'm so glad you're here, Paris. It means the world to me."

"I'm going to stay all night, Belle. I would tell you to go home and get some rest but I know you won't."

"You're right about that."

"I'll bring you a pillow and a blanket after I check on my other patient." Paris left the room, heading to Cindy Trollinger.

"My shift ends in twenty minutes. I'll go get us something from the diner to eat." Shane's eyes never left Juan. His concern for him nearly moved her to tears. "What would you like, Belle?"

"Anything." She'd planned on breaking up with him and Corey tonight, but the snake had derailed that plan.

After seeing how Shane and Corey were with Juan, she wasn't sure how she could bring herself to end it with them. Ever.

She knew in her heart it was wrong to let it go on like this. Maybe Amber was right. Maybe she just needed to tell them her truth. Maybe it would work out. Maybe they would be okay with adopting. *That's a ton of "maybes," Belle.* But she just couldn't bring herself to take away the chance for Shane and Corey to father their own children. It would be completely selfish of her to do so. They would choose her no matter what. But that wouldn't be fair to them. Telling them she couldn't have children wouldn't dissuade them one bit. She had to find another way to end it with them. It was the best thing to do.

I'll wait for just the right time to break it off. Now is not that time.

Doc Ryder came in with Juan's chart in his hand. "It's good to see my patient resting," he said in a hushed tone.

"Paris just checked his vitals," Corey told him.

"I see that here. Good. I won't disturb him. Belle, why don't we go out in the hall and I'll give you an update on his condition."

"I'll stay with Juan. I'm still on break," Shane said. "I'm sure Amber and Corey want to hear what Doc has to say, too. You can fill me in later."

Belle leaned over and kissed him. "Thank you."

Out in the hall, they found Gretchen and Ethel talking to Jason. He was standing guard at Cindy's room, which was next to Juan's. The two sweet women rushed to her side.

"How are you holding up, dear?" Gretchen asked Belle.

"I'll know how to answer you after Doc tells me Juan is going to be okay."

Doc smiled. "He is going to be fine, Belle, thanks to your quick thinking. Are you okay with me talking about Juan's treatment in front of everyone."

"Screw HIPAA rules, Doc. These are my friends and family. They can hear everything."

"Excellent. Juan's vitals are stable. He's responding to the antivenom perfectly. The swelling in his arm hasn't increased and I expect it to begin to go down in the next few days. His lungs are clear. His heart is strong. We're going to keep a close eye on him, though I'm very confident that he's going to be back to dragon hunting very soon."

Belle had been holding back her tears for so long, but hearing Doc's words caused them to fall from her eyes.

Corey hugged Belle, and she leaned into his strength.

Amber's voice shook. "Thank God."

Ethel and Gretchen were wiping their eyes.

Doc smiled. "I want to keep our little hero here for a few days."

Trollinger came out of her room with Paris. They both walked over to her, with Jason close behind.

Cindy walked right in front of Belle.

Corey pulled her in tighter, taking a step back from the woman.

A frown appeared on Cindy's face for a split second but disappeared when she turned her attention back to Belle. "How's your little boy doing?"

"Doc assures me he's going to be okay."

"That's great news. I told Paris to stop checking in on me. I'm not sick. She needs to spend all her time with Juan." Cindy held up her pack of cigarettes. "Time for a smoke break. It always clears my head. Belle, I'll check in on your boy tonight. You look like you could use some rest."

"That's okay. I'm not going anywhere."

"Neither am I." Corey's stare on Cindy didn't waiver.

"Seems I need to get more pillows and blankets." Paris grinned. "I'll be back in a flash." She left.

"Well, time for my evening break." Cindy turned to Jason. "You coming, Mr. Bodyguard?"

The sheriff didn't smile. "Yes."

Trollinger and Jason went to the end of the hallway that led outside.

Belle turned to Amber. "You should go home, Sis. I'm sure the boys are anxious, especially Jake. I always tuck them in. I just can't tonight."

"I'll do it, Belle. Don't worry. If you need me, no matter what time, call me. Promise."

"I promise."

"You have our numbers, Belle." Gretchen smiled. "We're here for you, too."

Ethel added, "Don't hesitate to call us."

"Thank you. I will. But I'm sure Corey, Shane, and I have things covered."

Corey, Shane, and I? The words came out as naturally as could be. She was surprised how right they felt on her lips. "Please tell everyone thanks for coming and showing their support."

Doc put his arm around Gretchen and Ethel's shoulders. "Belle, if you don't mind, I'll fill everyone in on Juan's condition. Then I can send them all home."

"I don't mind."

"That's good," Doc said. "I've already got wind that Juan is going to be on the front page of tomorrow's *Destiny Daily*."

She smiled. "He'll love that."

"Seriously, Belle. My brother had a snakebite last year and we pulled him through just fine. We'll do the same for Juan."

"Thank you, Doc."

Leading Gretchen and Ethel to the courtroom, Doc walked down the hallway the opposite direction Cindy and Jason had left.

Amber gave her a hug. "I love you, Sis."

"I love you, too."

Her sister followed Doc and the ladies, leaving Belle alone with Corey.

"Honey, I'm going to put you in the recliner. After we finish eating whatever Shane brings us, you're going to close your eyes." Corey kissed her on the forehead. "I'll take the first shift with our boy. You need to get a little sleep. I know you are exhausted."

God, he was such a loving man, always looking out for her. "Corey, I don't know what I would've done if you hadn't been there."

He smiled. "I was there, baby. By your side. That's where you and I belong. Together."

She felt tingles all over her body. *I'm in way too deep.* "Let's go back in."

He nodded and opened the door.

Belle walked in and the first thing she saw was Juan smiling.

"Once I get your hero badge, I want you to wear it everywhere." Shane was leaning over the bed, holding Juan's unbitten hand. "I want to make sure everyone shows you the respect and honor you deserve. You saved a life today. You've got the courage of ten men in my estimation, son."

Her heart swelled in her chest for Shane.

Juan spotted her. "Mom, Shane is going to get me a hero badge to wear."

"I heard." She moved next to Shane, gazing down at their little champion.

Corey moved to her other side. "Guess what, Juan?"

His eyes were wide with wonder. "What?"

"You're going to be on the front page of the paper tomorrow."

"I am?"

"You are."

Belle leaned down and kissed Juan. "Close your eyes, baby." She pulled up his covers, like she did every night. "Time to go to sleep."

"I love you, Mom."

"I love you, honey."

Chapter Eleven

Shane stood in the hallway with Corey, their parents, and sister just outside Juan's room. "Doc says it will be another day or two before he releases our boy."

"It's been three days, and Juan is fit to be tied." Corey smiled. "Christmas is in a few days and he wants to be home."

"I bet he does," Dad Curtis said.

Her mother smiled. "Juan reminds me of you two when you were that age."

"Oh boy, Mom. That means they've got their hands full, doesn't it?" Phoebe stood next to Jason, who, like Shane and Corey, had been relieved from guard duty thanks to the arrival of the three new agents.

Once Juan was back in full commission, Shane and Corey would return to the rotation, but Jason would not. Black had determined that with his other duties as sheriff, it was best to let Jason off the hook.

There had been no new developments on the Kip Lunceford issue. Nothing. Nada. Black had mentioned to Trollinger that he wanted to move her to the Dream Hotel because it had been so quiet. Cindy had seemed frightened by the prospect.

He glanced over at Trollinger's door where Jo and Brock Grayson, one of the new agents, were standing. He'd not had any time to get to know Brock or the other two, since he, Corey, and Belle hadn't left Juan's side the entire time, but they seemed like really great guys.

"How is Belle holding up?" Jason asked.

"Good." He smiled. "She's asleep now, thank God."

His mom looked at her watch. "Ten in the morning. I bet she's having trouble sleeping at all."

"That's true." Corey nodded. "Any movement or moan from Juan at whatever hour, she jumps to her feet to make sure he is okay. She's so good with him."

"She's his mother. It doesn't matter if she gave birth to him or not, he's deep in her heart. Of course, she's good with him." Their mom grabbed both their hands. "That little hero is in your hearts, too, isn't he?"

He and Corey nodded.

"That's because you're his dads, boys." Dad Eddie grinned. "It was hard to find a damn paper that next morning. You two bought them all up."

"So, Belle is his mom and you are his dads. You know what my next question is, don't you?" Their mom never did beat around the bush. "When are you going to ask Belle to marry you?"

"It's complicated, Mom." Shane turned to Corey, who was clearly in agreement. They'd talked over the past few days about how to proceed with Belle.

"She's a woman, son." Dad Curtis put his hand on his shoulder. "That's the definition of complicated."

"Hush up, Curtis." His mom smiled. "But your dad is right. My gender is difficult to understand sometimes. Tell us what's going on with your sweet Belle."

He and Corey shared with them how Belle had been holding back. They knew she cared for them but they also knew something was troubling her because she wouldn't open up to them.

"She might even break up with us." Shane's gut tightened at the thought.

Phoebe shook her head. "I don't believe that. Sometimes a woman says one thing but in her heart she feels another. I know."

"It's obvious she's in love with you both." Their mom smiled. "If she wasn't, she would've asked you to leave Juan's room. She hasn't. In fact, she's been clinging to you for dear life. Everyone in town sees it."

Dad Eddie turned to him and Corey. "What is in your heart for her, boys?"

"She's the one, Dad." Corey put his arm around his shoulder. "Our true love."

Shane nodded. "We couldn't bear not having her in our lives."

Dad Curtis jumped in. "Then don't let that happen. You've got to get her to see that future you want to build with her and Juan. No matter what, you have to help her overcome her doubts and fears."

Their mom grabbed their hands and squeezed. "She loves you. All you have to do is get her to open up. It's not going to be easy, but it's what you must do."

"Communication is the key to a relationship, brothers." Phoebe leaned into Jason. "Don't hold back like I did. I lost so much time with this one and his brothers. I would hate that to happen to you."

Shane turned to Corey. "I'm all in."

"So am I."

Their mom wiped her eyes. "If you'd like Grandma's engagement ring to give Belle, it's yours."

"Mom, I think that would be perfect." His mother's two dads had it made with two gold bands intertwined together. That ring symbolized so many things. Love. Family. Future.

Corey nodded, squeezing their mom. "We will be needing that ring soon. You'll see."

"What do you think of our boys, honey?" Dad Curtis asked.

"I'm so proud of them. They will make Belle very happy."

Shane and Corey walked back into Juan's room, determined to possess the woman of their dreams.

* * * *

Drinking hot chocolate, Belle sat on the back steps of the courthouse with Amber. The ground was covered in a thin blanket of snow that had fallen last night.

"God, that woman must have quite the addiction to nicotine." Amber pointed at the ashtray that Cindy had filled to overflowing with lipstick-covered butts. "How often does she come out here to smoke?"

"Not that I've been keeping tabs, but I think about twice an hour at least." Belle bet the woman was just bored. "It's hard on anyone to be cooped up for as long as she has. Thanks for coming. This is a nice break."

"You need more than a quick break, Sis. That's the real reason I wanted to talk to you alone."

"Amber, your ulterior motives always get me into trouble." Belle grinned, recalling one night when her sister had convinced her to sneak out of the house. Their parents had caught them and grounded them for a week. She missed those times very much.

"You're exhausted. You've only left this place to take a bath, and then you're always in a rush to get back."

"He's my son. My place is here."

"I know that, Belle, but Juan is fine. Any day now, Doc will be releasing him. You need a break. A real break. I want you to go with Shane and Corey and have some lunch. Just get out of here. I will stay with Juan. I don't want to see you back until tonight."

"Hey. Have you forgotten that I'm the older sister, not you?"

"How can I forget, Belle? You're always reminding me." Amber smiled. "I love you, and you know I'm right about this."

She shrugged, though the idea of getting away and clearing her head appealed to her.

"Stop being stubborn."

"Me? I'm never stubborn." She laughed, knowing that was hardly the case. "Okay. You win. I will have lunch with Shane and Corey." Her heart skipped a couple of beats. She knew she still had to talk with them.

* * * *

Corey poured Belle another glass of wine. "You look gorgeous in my robe, baby."

She sat on the sofa next to Shane. "With wet hair? I doubt that." She smiled. "You and Shane look nice in your shorts and T-shirts."

"I sure needed my shower." Shane smiled.

"Would you like some dessert, sweetheart?" Corey was glad to see her so at ease, though he could still sense something brewing under the surface of calm. "I think we have some ice cream in the freezer."

She shook her head. "I'm so full from the delicious lunch you guys made for me."

Corey sat down next to her, opposite Shane. "We like spoiling you."

"I really appreciate all you've done for me. It's been a tough few days." She smiled. "I feel so relaxed now, knowing that Juan is okay." Her eyes lowered and she twisted her hands together.

He touched her on the cheek. "Baby, what's troubling you?"

"You have nothing to fear here, sweetheart." Shane grabbed her hand.

She nodded. "This is so hard to say. I know it's past time, but I'm not sure how to tell you since you've been so wonderful to me."

"We've come too far to be left in the dark." Though it did seem she was opening up to him and Shane some, her tone told him she still was bent on ending the relationship. He looked over at Shane, who was clearly sensing the same thing. "We need to know now, Belle."

"I can't thank you enough for all you've done for Juan and me. I don't know what I would've done without you since the rattlesnake bit him. You're good for Juan. His face lights up whenever you are around." Her lips began to tremble slightly. "What I'm about to say, please, don't let that change how you feel about him."

His gut tightened. "Nothing you can say will change that, Belle."

"He is our son," Shane stated firmly. "Stop beating around the bush, baby."

"I'm sorry." She closed her eyes. "This is the hardest thing I've ever had to do."

He kissed her cheek. "Spill it, baby. What do you have to say?"

She opened her eyes and took a deep breath. "I just want us to be friends."

Shane's face darkened. "Friends? Is that what you really want?"

"I'm sorry, but I think it would be best."

Corey locked his eyes on her, demanding her full attention. "Are you breaking up with us, Belle? Is that what you came to say?"

"Yes." Tears welled in her eyes. "I wish it could be different, but there are things about me you don't know."

Corey put his hand on her shoulder, knowing the time had finally arrived to unlock her secrets. "What things don't we know?"

She shook her head. "It doesn't matter."

Shane's hand landed on her leg. "But you are wrong, Belle. It matters to us."

"You want to end the best thing that has ever been in our lives. We deserve to know the reason." Using the deepest register of his voice, Corey asked, "Do you understand?"

She gulped. "Yes, but—"

"No 'buts.'"

Shane cupped her chin. "You. Will. Tell. Us."

Her eyes widened, and she blurted out. "I can't have children." She blinked, brought her hands up to her mouth and started sobbing. "I can't...I can't...I can't give you babies."

Oh my God, my poor angel. "You think that changes anything about how I feel about you? It doesn't." He pulled her in tight. "Not one fucking bit."

Carrying that kind of burden, no wonder she'd been holding back for so long.

"You've already given us a child, baby." Shane squeezed her from the other side. "Juan is our son. We are his dads. I've never felt so complete in my life. I'm in love with you, Belle. I can't let you go."

"You took the words right out of my mouth, bro." He brushed the hair out of her eyes. "Sweetheart, you have given me more than I ever dreamed of. I can't imagine a single day without you in it. I love you. I will always love you."

Her tears subsided. "And I love you, but I'm not sure that's enough. And what about your parents? Don't they deserve grandchildren?"

"We already told you how we feel about Juan." Corey held her even tighter, hoping to quell her trembles. "Mom and Dads love him, too."

"Corey and I have already talked about the three of us adopting him. Time to let the state of Colorado know what is already in our hearts."

"Listen to my brother, baby. We're a family. There are plenty of kids who need good homes."

Shane nodded. "Look at all those boys at your sister's ranch. We can have a house full of children. As many as we like."

The smile that spread across her face thrilled both him and Corey. "Are you sure?"

"Beyond a shadow of a doubt, baby." He kissed her, claiming her as his own, sending his tongue past her lips. She wrapped her arms around his neck, an early act of submission that caused his cock to stir.

He released her.

Shane pressed his mouth to hers. She moaned sweetly as their kiss ended.

Back and forth, they passed the woman of their dreams, kissing all her tears away.

Her face became beautifully flushed, causing his hunger to grow and grow.

He ran his hand down her arm. "I want you, baby. I want you now."

Shane nodded. "Now who is taking the words out of whose mouth?"

Corey lifted her off the sofa. "Let's take this discussion to the bedroom."

She wrapped her arms around his neck. "I love that idea, honey."

With Shane following, Corey carried Belle into his bedroom. This was only the beginning of a long and happy life together.

Chapter Twelve

Belle looked into the eyes of Shane and Corey.

They love me. They really, really love me.

Corey lowered her to her feet. "Take off *my* robe." It was clearly a command not a request.

Unable to resist, she let the robe slip off her shoulders to the floor, which left her without a stitch of clothing.

"Very nice." Shane's face was full of lust as he scanned her body freely.

Corey nodded, a wicked grin spreading across his handsome face. "You can say that again."

Her two sexy men stood before her, their muscled chests rising and falling like two hungry predators who had just captured their prey. Being their morsel was something she wanted more than anything.

"On your knees, baby." Shane's voice rumbled deep from inside.

Corey's eyes narrowed in hot lust.

Their dominance was washing over her like a powerful salve.

She lowered herself to the floor, placing her knees together. "Like this?"

"Exactly like that." Corey shed his shorts.

He looked like a god staring down at her with his long, thick cock erect.

Shane undressed in a flash. Just like Corey, his muscled frame was divine, his massive dick upright.

She was flawed, a woman unable to bring life into the world. Her two wonderful, loving men didn't see her as lesser. Not at all. To them she was perfection, and that made her feel feminine and alive more than any other time in her life.

With all her being, she wanted to please them. Gazing at their ten-inch shafts, she licked her lips seductively. "I'd like to taste you."

"Is that right?" Corey stepped forward. "I would love to feel your pretty lips around my cock, so I guess we're both in luck."

Shane nodded, moving behind her. His hands landed on her shoulder, creating a kind of restraint, reminding her that they were in control. Exactly as she wanted them to be.

"You've been pushing us away for too long." Corey moved right in front of her, positioning his cock a fraction of an inch from her lips. So thick and long, it nearly reached his navel. "Now that we have you, baby, we're going to make sure that you never want to push us away again."

A warm tingle spread from her belly through the rest of her body. She vibrated like a livewire as her desperation for them expanded inside her. She looked up at him. "May I taste you now?"

He smiled and touched her cheek. "Damn, you are more than I dreamed was possible. Yes, you may taste me now. You may wrap that gorgeous mouth around my cock. You may suck on me to your heart's content. If I tell you to stop, you will. Understand?"

He clearly had something else in mind, and that realization only drove up the pressure already building inside her. "I understand."

Feeling Shane's hands glide up and down her back, urging her on, Belle wrapped her fingers around Corey's cock. It was warm to the touch and so very hard. A tiny glistening pearl sat on the tip.

She licked it up, savoring Corey's salty slickness on her lips. "I love the way you taste."

Shane's throaty chuckle gave her sweet shivers. "Saucy little thing, aren't you?"

"I wouldn't have her any other way, Shane."

"Me either. She is perfect just in every way."

Their awe-filled praise made her heart swell in her chest.

Corey's hand moved to the back of her neck. "Show me what you can do with that mouth of yours, sweetheart. Don't make me wait another second."

His wicked impatience was something that excited her. Pumping his shaft, she grabbed his heavy balls with her other hand and slid her lips down his cock.

"That feels great, baby."

His praise spurred her on. She bobbed up and down his dick, feeling it hit the back of her throat.

She glanced up at Corey, keeping his cock in her mouth. His eyes were open, but only barely.

"Fuck. So good. Damn."

"Show him, Belle." Shane kissed her between the shoulder blades. "Drive him crazy."

Shane reached around her, his fingers dancing lightly over her breasts. Her nipples tingled and her pussy began to ache.

Continuing to suck on him, Belle could feel Corey's heartbeat on her lips. *Thump. Thump. Thump.* She matched the rhythm of their pulses, sliding up and down his shaft, sucking until her cheeks hollowed out.

Shane tweaked her nipples, creating two tingling lines that shot down her body, merging into a swirling ball of need between her legs.

Shane's lips feathered against her neck. "Spread your knees for me."

She obeyed instantly, continuing to worship Corey with her mouth.

Shane moved his hand to her wet pussy, threading his fingers through her swollen folds. "I'm going to drink this sweet cream, baby. Every drop. Corey and I are going to fill you up and make you come again and again until you think you can't take more. But you will. Much more."

Oh God. Yes.

When his thumb pressed on her throbbing clit, she became delirious from the expanding pressure inside her. With her hair hanging over Corey's cock, she sped up her oral devotion.

"You're about there, baby." Shane's lusty tone hit something deep inside her, something that needed the dominance only he and Corey could give, something ready to surrender all to them. "Come for us, Belle. Come now."

Like gasoline to a flame, his words and touch unleashed blinding sensations. The quake began in her pussy but spread out through her body, igniting every nerve ending. She continued sucking on Corey, since he hadn't told her to stop. She wanted to bring him the same mind-blowing pleasure she was feeling.

"Ahhh." Corey's handsome face tightened and his eyes finally closed. He grabbed her by the hair and she swallowed his cock as he shot his seed down her throat.

Shane pressed her throbbing clit again, doubling her already intense orgasm. Dizzy from the overpowering release they'd given her, she drank down all of Corey's hot liquid.

The closeness she felt to Shane and Corey was like nothing she'd ever experienced before. They had opened her up and she'd shared her darkest truth. There wasn't anyone she felt more connected to, anyone she wanted to be with more, anyone she wanted to spend the rest of her life with.

Corey's fingers caressed the side of her face. "You beautiful creature. I'm so glad you came into my life."

They both lifted her off the floor and onto the bed.

She trembled as Shane placed his hands on her thighs and Corey feathered his fingers over her taut nipples.

"God, you smell so good." Shane's breath skated over her swollen folds, causing another round of pressure to grow inside her.

Corey gently massaged her breast while licking the sensitive spots on her neck and shoulders.

When Shane dragged his tongue over her wet pussy, she fisted the sheets just to try to find some fingerhold on sanity. It didn't work. "Oh God. Yes."

Each swipe of their tongues, each caress of their fingers, each blast of their hot breath drove her mad with want.

"Sweet. So very sweet." Shane circled her throbbing clit with his tongue while sending a finger into her channel. "You like me finger fucking you, baby?"

"Oh God. Please." She shifted her hips up, trying to find the relief she needed so badly. But none came, only more delirious pressure, building and building and building.

"What a pretty pussy, so tight, so sweet, so mine." Shane bathed her pussy with his hot, manly mouth.

Corey teethed her nipples, sending new sparks throughout her trembling body. Every inch of her—lips, nipples, clit—pulsed hot and hard. She needed to explode, needed relief, needed release.

"You taste so fucking good." Shane groaned and continued his oral conquest of her sex. She felt his fingers part her labia. His tongue went up and down every inch of her pussy. She could hear his lusty slurps and that only added to her craze.

Inching closer to ecstasy, she clawed at Corey, needing to feel his flesh on her fingertips. The sting his greedy mouth gave her aching nipples morphed into sweet bits of pleasure. All she could think was she wanted more. More from her two men. More lovemaking. More everything. More tomorrows with them.

When Shane captured her clit between his lips, delivering the perfect amount of squeeze, she came with a scream. The immense pressure released into a swarm of sensations that spread out through her body.

"Drown me in your juices, baby." Shane drank from her pussy like it was the most precious fountain in the world.

Tremors shook her from head to toe as her orgasm continued, sending her into a dizzy state of rapture. She closed her eyes, trying to steady anything—her breathing, her body, her heart—but it was impossible. Riding out the sensations, focusing her mind, was proving difficult, though she was aware of Corey and Shane moving her on her side between them.

Corey was behind her and she could feel him spreading the cheeks of her ass.

Shane grabbed her hand and sent it between his legs.

She wrapped her fingers around his monstrous shaft.

"That's my baby. Feel my dick." His lips feathered over her neck. "You understand how we're going to fuck you tonight, don't you?"

She nodded and chewed on her lower lip as the pressure returned with even greater ferocity.

Corey applied lubricant to her anus.

"Yes. Oh God. Please. I've got to have you inside me."

"And you will get your wish, sweetheart." Corey rimmed her with his slicked up finger, making her tremble like mad. "I am going to claim this sweet ass." He sent a finger past the tight ring, and she burned with pleasure.

"More. Please. More."

The tip of Shane's cock pressed on her pussy, driving her crazy.

Corey ruthlessly fucked her ass with his fingers.

"Please. Please." She ached to have their cocks inside her.

Shane grinned wickedly. "Please what, Belle?"

"I need you both."

"Need us to do what, baby?" His face was hot with lust but his words were so calm and steady.

His self-control amazed her.

She was out of her mind with desire. "I want you inside me. I want your cocks inside me. I want it so badly. Please. Please. Please."

Shane smiled. "That's all we wanted to hear, sweetheart."

He and Corey kept her sandwiched between them as they rolled her facedown on top of Shane.

Shane shifted slightly until the head of his cock was positioned perfectly. He groaned and plunged into her pussy, stretching her so nicely. Her body was still oscillating from the orgasms they'd given her already. She wondered if she could manage another, but the intimate, overwhelming connection she felt with her two men spurred her on.

Feeling the head of Corey's dick start to push into her ass took her breath away.

"It's okay, sweetheart," Corey whispered. "Relax."

She closed her eyes as he inched his massive cock deeper into her ass.

"Love this sweet, tight ass." Corey groaned, triggering her to action.

She shifted back into him, taking more of his dick into her depths. "Oh God. So full. So incredibly full."

"You feel so good, baby." Shane thrust into her.

"God, you are so hot." Corey's tone deepened to a rumble.

She clawed at Shane's shoulders as he and Corey thrust into her body. They were stretching her, causing her breaths to divide in half with every plunge. Deliciously dizzy, she felt every nerve ending inside her fire blistering hot.

Corey reached around her and stroked her clit, sending her over the edge into an orgasm she'd never had known was possible. Her body erupted like a supernova, exploding in every direction. Screaming at the violent and incredible release, she felt Corey stiffen behind her.

"Fuuck." He came in her ass.

Shane groaned, his eyes closing, as he sent his seed into her pussy.

Completely spent, she trembled and felt tears of joy roll down her cheeks.

My two Doms.

Chapter Thirteen

Belle walked between Shane and Corey into the courthouse. Her sister had been right about the need for a real break. Her heart was theirs, no doubt about it. She felt refreshed, thanks fully to her guys.

My guys? She was in deep. It felt so surreal.

They headed down the hallway to Juan's room. It was late. As expected, when they opened the door they found him fast asleep. Amber was sitting in the chair reading the latest book from Lexi Blake, another of her favorite authors. Her husband Emmett sat in the other chair, reading a magazine.

Amber looked up and smiled. *I know she can tell what happened.* She turned to Emmett and whispered, "Do you mind if I have a little talk with my sis before we go?"

I can't keep anything from Amber.

"Sure, sweetheart. Take as long as you like. Shane, Corey, and I can hold down the fort."

Her sister stood and walked up to Shane and Corey. "Thank you for finally getting her away from here."

Shane smiled. "Our pleasure, Amber."

Corey held the door for both of them and they walked out into the hall.

Dylan and Nicole were guarding Trollinger, so she and Amber headed the other direction, out the door to the back step, the same place this morning her sister had convinced her to take a much-needed break.

"You look amazing, Belle." Amber grabbed her hand. "Now tell me everything."

"Amber, I just rested and got to take a shower."

"You're avoiding the real truth, Sis. I want to hear all about it. Everything."

"Okay, nosy." She laughed. "We had sex. It was amazing. It was different than anything I've ever experienced. I only know a little about the BDSM lifestyle, but I think they were trying to introduce me to it. They were in such control, trying to please my every need. I felt things I've never felt before, Sis. It was mind-blowing."

"I agree with you, Belle. My guys have shown me things I never dreamed possible. Shane and Corey are clearly ready to do the same for you. Did you tell them?"

She nodded. "They told me it didn't matter. They even talked about wanting to adopt Juan."

Amber put her arm around her shoulder. "Your little sister is quite smart, don't you think."

"You are wonderful." Belle looked up at the mountain peaks that were illuminated by the full moon. They looked much bigger here than they had at the guys' lookout spot. It had started to snow again. Doubt began to creep out of the shadows of her mind. "I'm still not sure this is the right thing to do. It's not fair to them."

"Belle, please stop. Why do you do this to yourself? They love you. Love is all you need. Love is all any of us need. It will see you through whatever challenges come your way. Don't you love them?"

"With all my heart. That's what's killing me." She sighed, and her breath floated out in a fog in the chilly December air. "I want to be with them. I do. They make me so happy. But how can I take away something so precious from them?"

"Sis, they told you it didn't matter. Why can't you accept that?"

"Even if I can now, what happens after several years pass? How can I look at their beautiful faces and know I'm the reason they were denied children of their own? I can't bring myself to break it off with them, but I can't imagine staying either. I'm so confused."

"Enough is enough, Belle. Like Mom always said, quit borrowing trouble."

"But—"

They heard footsteps heading their way from the trees off to their left.

Amber looked the direction of the noise. She whispered. "We better get inside, Sis. No one should be out here at this hour."

Belle completely agreed, and they went back inside.

* * * *

When Belle and Amber walked back into Juan's room, Corey could see in both their eyes that something had startled them.

Emmett and Shane must've thought the same thing because they each stood up.

"What's wrong, baby?" Emmett wrapped his arms around Amber.

"We heard a cracking noise in the ice."

Corey put his arm around Belle. "You okay?"

She nodded. "With everything going on with Kip's sister, we decided it was best to come back inside."

"You did the right thing, baby." Shane grabbed Belle's hand. "Did you see anyone?"

"No. The noise came from that cluster of trees near the parking lot." She sighed. "Maybe our imaginations were getting the better of us. It might have just been an animal."

"You did the right thing, girls." Corey turned to Emmett. "If you'll stay with Amber and Belle, Shane and I can go check it out."

Emmett nodded, opening his coat slightly to reveal to him and Shane that he was armed. No surprise, since most in Destiny never left home without a gun.

He and Shane walked out the door, the only way into the room.

Shane turned to Dylan and Nicole. "We might have an intruder outside. Belle and Amber heard something suspicious out back. Corey and I are going to check it out."

Dylan nodded. "I'll check the main courtroom and the front of the building."

"Should I notify the rest of the team?" Nicole brought out her ROC.

"Wait until we know for sure." Corey pulled his gun out of his holster. "It's late. No sense in sounding the alarm until we know if there is a threat or not."

She nodded. "I'll stay here. Send me a message as soon as you know."

He and Shane headed out the back, weapons drawn. Dylan did the same out the front.

Cautiously, Corey walked out of the building, scanning in every direction. The snow was coming down in thick, wet flakes.

Once they got to the trees, they saw several fresh footprints that were quickly being erased by the snow.

Shane bent down, staring at the tracks. "You follow them that way." He pointed to the street. "I'll go this direction." Without a word, Shane headed to the side of the courthouse.

Corey followed the vanishing tracks across First Street before losing them completely. *Fuck.*

Shane and Dylan met up with him back at the trees. All the tracks they'd discovered were completely wiped out. Even their own.

"Whoever it was is long gone." Shane holstered his gun. "It might've been a local."

"Or it might've been someone on Lunceford's payroll, bro."

"Instead of checking the perimeter every hour, it's time to increase that to every quarter hour." Dylan pulled out his ROC. "I sent a message to Nicole and the rest of the team with what we found."

"Good." When Corey was first recruited by Black for Shannon's Elite, he had balked at the idea. But now, he couldn't imagine being anywhere else. He trusted Dylan and the others with his life. "Until we know for sure whose footprints were in the snow, we've got to be on our guard."

"Absolutely." Shane's face darkened. "I still don't trust Trollinger."

"We've ran every search possible and everything about her story pans out," Dylan stated flatly. "She's been in Destiny for several weeks and those footprints are the first sign of trouble we've had."

When they came to the back steps, Shane stopped in his tracks. "Hold up, fellas."

Corey looked at his brother, wondering what was on his mind.

"You have something?" Dylan asked.

"Only an idea. Come with me." Shane headed to the parking lot at the back of the courthouse. He walked over to Cindy Trollinger's car, which was the only one parked there at this hour. He bent down, checking the block heater under the vehicle that had been placed there since the woman's arrival.

Corey was stumped. "What are we doing here, bro?"

"Trollinger made it a point to ask that her car be taken care of. Hell, at least once during her smoke breaks she asks one of us to turn the engine over. Don't you find it odd that she's that concerned about her car?"

"Yes, but everything she's told us has checked out, Shane."

"It's not like she's planning on going anywhere, or so she tells us. Kind of suspicious, don't you think?"

Dylan nodded. "You are definitely Langley trained, Blue."

"Whoever made those footprints might be working with her or coming for her. It doesn't matter which. Black and Jason have kept their eyes on Silver Spoon Bridge for any cars ever since we learned she was Lunceford's sister. My bet is the footprint guy either arrived in town the same time Cindy showed up and he's been here the whole time, hiding out, waiting to pounce once he gets the go-ahead from whoever is pulling his strings. Or he got here walking the shoreline or by boat. Either way, I believe this mystery man is tied to Lunceford."

"Your theory makes a whole lot of sense to me." Corey couldn't have asked for a better brother, a better friend. "We need to tell Black about what you've come up with. I'm sure he'll want to get some eyes on the shoreline and beach."

Shane nodded. "And as a safety net, I think putting a tracker on Trollinger's car is a must."

"Brilliant idea, Blue," Dylan said.

"I agree, bro." They all knew that if the mystery fucker tried to bolt with or without Cindy in her car, they would have him.

* * * *

It was 9:00 p.m., nearly twenty-four hours after Belle and her sister had heard the cracking of the ice. Trying to convince Shane and Corey that it only made sense for her to go with Paris into Cindy's room for the final round was proving difficult.

Juan had his headphones on and was playing his video games, so they could talk freely.

"Trollinger isn't even sick." Corey's jaw was locked. The guy had a stubborn streak a mile long.

"Paris still has to change her sheets. Besides, if I stop going in with Paris, Cindy is going to get suspicious. You still don't think she's working with Lunceford, do you?"

Shane shrugged. "Maybe she gets suspicious or maybe she doesn't. We still aren't thrilled with you going in. If you insist, one of us will go in with you."

"What do you think Cindy can do to me? Bite me? She doesn't have any weapons. There's no way in or out of the room except by the door. If you go in with me, that will also tip her off." Knowing that they both were only trying to protect her, she decided to make her case another way. "Besides, you promised Doc to take care of Paris. Is it safe for her to go into the room alone?"

Corey sighed. "Damn it, Belle. You're too smart for your own good. You should've been an attorney instead of a nurse. With your talent at arguing I doubt you would've lost a single case."

"Good. Case closed."

Shane pulled her in close. "You will go in with Paris, not alone."

Paris walked into the room. "Sorry. Do I need to come back?"

Belle shook her head. "Your timing couldn't be more perfect."

Corey placed his hand on the back of her neck. "The first sign of trouble, you call in Jonas and Cooper and then you come get us. Understand?"

"Can you be more overprotective? I don't think so." She grinned. "Yes, your majesties, I understand."

Shane cupped her chin. "Mock all you want, but if you're not back in ten minutes, we're coming to get you."

"I don't doubt that at all." She kissed both Shane and Corey. "I'll be fine."

Juan looked up from his game.

She motioned for him to take off his headset.

"Mom, just ten more minutes. Please."

She smiled, happy to see him nearly completely healed. "Put it away. You can watch television but no more video games. They always keep you up too late."

He nodded and turned to Shane and Corey. "May I pick the show?"

"Of course," they both said in unison.

She left the room, following her friend out into the hallway.

Paris stood right in front of her. "That was intense, Belle."

"Shane and Corey are the definition of intense. How's your other patient doing?"

"Calling Cindy a patient isn't quite correct, is it? She's fine, though a little stir-crazy I think. Who wouldn't be?" She pointed at Jonas Ward and Cooper Ross, who were standing guard for this shift. "It's like she's a prisoner."

"I think Shannon's Elite is trying to protect her the best they can."

The sound of ice cracking that Belle and Amber had heard last night had put everyone on edge again. Lunceford, the town's most wanted criminal, was still completely off the radar. All the citizens of Destiny felt the frustration of the entire team.

"Belle, Doc told me he's going to release Juan day after tomorrow. Doc knows it's a little early, but since you are a nurse he feels confident that he'll be in good hands."

"Juan's doing so well. Keeping him still will be quite the job, but thankfully, I've got Corey and Shane to help me."

"Yes, you do." Paris winked.

"Don't start that now. Please."

"Start what?" Paris shrugged. "Let's get Cindy some fresh sheets."

"Subject change? So like you."

"If you need to talk about your two guys, I'm here for you. You know that, don't you?"

She grabbed Paris's hands. "Yes. I know. You're a good friend."

Her friend's green eyes locked in on her. "I thought things were going well with you three."

"They are. Too good. Once we're done in Cindy's room, maybe I can get my two overprotective bruisers to allow me to grab a cup of coffee with you. I can tell you all about it."

"You've got a deal, Belle."

Belle took a deep breath as they stepped up to Cindy's door. The woman seemed to trust her. Maybe today might be the time Kip's sister would share something that could be helpful for Black and the team.

Paris nodded to the two new agents, who were quite attractive. Belle knew from their talks that Paris only had eyes for the two Ryder brothers, Doc and Mick, though she protested otherwise.

They walked in.

Cindy was on the phone. Her face was flushed and her eyes were red. "I won't do that for you, you son of a bitch."

Belle and Paris rushed to her side.

"The line went dead." Cindy turned to Belle. "Kip found me."

Her heart skipped several beats as Belle held out her hand. "Give me your phone."

The woman seemed to be in a daze. "Lunceford has leukemia. He told me he's coming for me. He wants my bone marrow."

"Give me your phone, Cindy. Now." Belle had to get it to Shane and Corey, had to tell them about this new development, had to save her town from Lunceford.

Cindy nodded and handed her the cell. "I don't know what to do."

"But I do." Belle turned around and headed to the two men she trusted more than anyone else in the world.

She rushed past Jonas and Cooper and into Juan's room. Juan was watching a John Wayne movie with Shane and Corey.

All three of them looked her way.

Shane stood. "That was fast."

"Mom, the movie just started." Juan smiled. "It's about kids who become cowboys. Do you want to watch it with us?"

"I do, but first, I need to talk to Shane and Corey." Juan had been through so much already. Even as brave and mature as her twelve-year-old boy was, she didn't want to scare him. "Give us a minute, sweetheart."

Shane and Corey didn't ask any questions before walking out the door with her.

"What's wrong, baby?" Shane always did seem to see into her.

"Cindy just got a phone call from Kip." She handed him Trollinger's cell. "The bastard has leukemia. He wants her to be his donor."

Corey's face darkened. "How does he know she's a match?"

"I doubt he does." Working in her ex's hematology practice had increased Belle's knowledge about the disease. She knew that siblings and family members increased the odds for a perfect match. "Cindy is likely his best chance."

Corey pulled out a device that she'd learned was called a ROC. "Dylan put a tracer on her cell. With any luck, we might have the origination point of the call."

"Honey, you did good. This might be the best chance we've had to catch Lunceford." Shane waved Jonas and Cooper over.

"What's up?" Jonas asked.

Shane and Corey filled them in on the call from Kip.

Cooper nodded. "Sounds like we need to up our game."

Corey looked at the screen of his ROC. "Black already knows about the call from Kip. He's on his way here now with the rest of the team."

Chapter Fourteen

Shane took Belle by the hand and led her out of the courthouse. Corey walked on the other side of their dream woman.

"Please, promise we won't be gone long." Belle's concern for Juan was just one of the things he loved about her.

"You call us overprotective." Shane grinned. "You should look in the mirror, baby."

"Doc is releasing Juan tomorrow, honey." Corey put his arm around her shoulders. "He is fine. Besides, Cooper and Jonas promised to keep an eye on him for us."

"I know, but I can't help it. He's my boy."

Corey nodded. "He's our boy, too."

"Don't forget that we promised to bring him sweet and sour chicken and as many fortune cookies as Mr. Phong would allow us to have." She smiled, but Shane sensed something behind her seemingly happy demeanor that troubled him.

She was still holding back. He and Corey both knew it. With Juan's release tomorrow, they'd decided now was the best time to confront her before her schedule got crazy.

He kissed her. "Let's walk to the Wok."

She grinned. "The snow looks beautiful in the park, doesn't it?"

"Yes, it does." He glanced over at the statue of the Blue Dragon, also known as Mother Dragon. She had a tuft of snow on her wings that only added to her regal stature.

They headed down South Street to their destination—Phong's Wok.

The place was empty save one table by the front door.

Wearing her deputy sheriff uniform, Nicole Flowers sat alone finishing her lunch. "I can't believe you finally convinced Belle to leave the courthouse. How did you do it?"

"We can be quite persuasive, deputy." Shane squeezed Belle's hand. "She needed to get some fresh air and stretch her legs. We weren't going to take no for an answer."

Nicole smiled and turned to Belle. "If these two are harassing you in any way, just let me know. I'll arrest them. Just say the word."

Belle grinned. "We're only here for the delicious Chinese food. That's all. Shane and Corey promised it would only be an hour. If they try to keep me longer, I'll definitely let you know."

"You've got a deal." Nicole had her ROC out, which impressed him.

Like the rest of the team, Nicole was working day and night to find something that would lead them to Lunceford. So far—nothing.

The mystery man's footprints hadn't helped them a bit. Neither had the knowledge that Kip allegedly wanted Cindy's bone marrow. Truthfully, they hadn't even been able to verify the bastard had leukemia. Dead ends were all they were finding on this case, and it was driving them all crazy.

Melissa Phong, Hiro's wife, came out of the back. "Sit anywhere you like."

Shane selected a booth at the far back corner of the restaurant.

He sat next to Belle, and Corey sat across from them.

Melissa brought them menus. "Belle, how's your little hero doing?"

"He's ready to get back to the ranch. Thank you for coming to the Boys Ranch opening. Your support means so much to us."

"Of course. The work you and your sister do with those boys is wonderful. Let me get you some jasmine tea and I'll give you a few minutes to decide on your meal."

Corey handed his menu back to her. "No need for me. You already know what I want."

Melissa smiled. "Chicken chow mein, right?"

"You got it."

The woman turned to Shane. "You always get orange pork or kung pao beef."

"Orange pork tonight." He had always treasured the matriarch of the Phong clan since he was a boy.

"Belle, you never stray from sesame chicken. Correct?"

"I wouldn't dream of it."

"I bet Juan told you to bring back fortune cookies, didn't he?"

"How do you keep everyone's favorite straight in your head, Melissa?"

"I'm smart, that's how." The woman laughed and headed back to the kitchen.

Shane turned to Belle. "Now that we're alone, it's time to tell you the real reason we brought you here."

"I thought we were here for lunch."

"True, but I'm known for not beating around the bush." He placed his hand over hers. "We had a great talk the other night. Corey and I felt like we have everything hashed out between us. But we can tell you are once again holding something back."

Corey leaned forward, taking her other hand. "We don't want any walls between us. We are family now. You are ours. Don't you trust us?"

She took a deep breath as her eyes welled up with tears. "It's not a matter of trust. I just don't want to hurt you."

"We know you can't have children, sweetheart." Shane hated seeing the suffering on her face. "We do not care. As we've said before, we have Juan. He's our son. We'll adopt."

"I know you feel that way now. What happens ten years from now? Will you look at me differently then? Will you regret your decision?" She began to tremble. "I love you both so much. I do not want to deny you that pleasure. I've been through this before. Did you know I was married once? A doctor. I cared for him but not even a fraction as much as I care for you. When I couldn't give him children we both knew what we'd had was over. It kills me to think of you out of my life, but every day I am falling even deeper in love with you." Her voice shook and turned to a whisper. "You're the most wonderful men I've ever known. Saying good-bye will destroy me, but you deserve a woman who can give you children."

"I love you, Belle. And I am going to go over this one more time." Shane touched her cheek. "But you hear me now. This is the last time we bring this up again."

"I agree with my brother, sweetheart." Corey leaned forward. "You are my heart, my soul mate, my everything. I won't spend a single day without you in my life."

Shane kissed her forehead. "You think our lives aren't full? My God, Belle, you and Juan have given us everything our hearts desire. Stop second-guessing the happiness we all feel. I know you've been through a lot. Losing your parents when you were so young must've been devastating. I bet you are always on guard whenever you get happy, expecting the next shoe to fall, the next tragedy to take over, the next heart to break. Baby, you don't have to worry any more. We will always be here for you. You are our forever."

"Get that through your pretty little head." Corey's tone deepened. He meant business. "We aren't going anywhere. We are here. Always. Stop trying to push us away, because you can't. Do you understand?"

Tears streamed down her face. "Yes. I understand. I love you so much. I will never bring it up again. I swear."

Corey leaned all the way over the table and grabbed Belle, crashing his mouth to hers. She moaned her surrender.

When his brother released her, Shane consumed her lips. Feeling her delicate hands on his face intoxicated him.

They heard the familiar buzzing sound of their ROCs.

Shane looked at his screen and saw the message from Black.

Urgent!

Grayson just discovered a boat filled with explosives on Lover's Beach.

Wolfe, Strange, and I are headed his way.

Ross and Ward, ensure Trollinger is buttoned up.

The rest of you stand by for orders.

Black

"Time to go to work, bro." Corey jumped up from the table. "Let's get our girl back to Juan's room."

Nicole walked over. "I just got Black's message."

Belle's eyes were wide. "What's going on?"

Corey said, "Looks like your footprint guy is making his move."

"I've got to get to my son."

"Exactly."

Melissa came over with their tea. "Leaving already?"

Corey nodded. "Sorry, but duty calls."

They all heard an explosion and ran to the door.

His and Corey's parents' diner was engulfed in flames.

Dread flattened him. *Are Mom and Dads inside?*

"Go," Belle screamed and took off for the courthouse.

"Just go to your parents. I'll make sure she gets to Juan." Nicole ran after Belle.

He and Corey bolted to the diner.

Shane's insides were being ripped to shreds.

* * * *

With every fiber of her being, Belle needed to get to Juan.

Thank God, he is in his room and not at the diner.

Nicole was close behind as she ran into the courthouse.

Belle turned down the hallway to Juan's room.

Her heart seized in her chest when she saw Cooper and Jonas on the floor at Cindy's door, both with gunshot wounds.

Another man, dressed in black, was dead on the floor next to them.

She ran to Juan's room. The door was open.

He's gone. Oh God. No!

* * * *

Being first on the scene, Corey ran into the burning building with Shane.

Their mother and several customers were pinned under debris in what was once the dining room.

"Mom, first," Shane said.

He nodded and they went into action.

She's breathing. Thank God.

Once they had her free, Shane carried her out.

Corey saw Desirae, one of the waitresses, with blood dripping from her mouth.

"I'm fine, Corey. Go check on everyone else." She was helping one of the customers to their feet.

The kitchen, the domain of his dads, was completely engulfed in flames.

* * * *

Belle ran out of Juan's room, crazed with panic. She had to find Juan.

Nicole was giving Jonas CPR. "One. Two. Three." She bent down and breathed for the man.

Belle stepped past them and opened Trollinger's door, hoping to find Juan with her—safe and sound.

The room was empty.

She wanted to scream.

She bent down over Cooper, who was mumbling something unintelligible.

"Where is he? Where is my Juan?"

Cooper closed his eyes. "Gone...away...back...she..." He groaned from the pain of his wound.

"Please, Cooper. Tell me. Help me find my son."

* * * *

Shane carried out the last person they could reach in the diner. No chance of getting back inside now. The volunteer fire department was trying to put out the flames but it was a total loss.

Doc, Paris, and Katy were caring for the victims with the help of Doc's brother Mick and other Destonians. His mom was in bad shape, but not life-threatening.

Corey walked up to him, choking and covered in ash. His brother didn't say a word but shook his head. He knew exactly what that meant. Corey hadn't found their dads or any of the other cooks. Had Dad Curtis and Dad Eddie been in the kitchen when the bomb went off? It was obvious that had been where it had been placed.

I will kill whoever did this.

* * * *

As Cooper lost consciousness, Belle felt her entire body go numb.

Nicole was continuing to give Jonas CPR.

Belle was completely shaken and didn't know where to turn, what to do.

Her cell buzzed.

It had to be Shane and Corey. *I need you.*

She read the text and realized it hadn't come from her guys.

Belle,
I've got Juan out back. He's safe. Come now.
Cindy

Without hesitation, Belle ran to get her son.

* * * *

Corey held his mother's hand.

Shane knelt on the other side of her.

Doc had told them she'd taken in a lot of smoke and her arm was broken, but nothing else. She was going to recover fully.

Corey kissed her forehead. "We're here, Mom."

Through the oxygen mask, he saw her smile, which broke his heart. What would happen to her once she learned they hadn't found Dad Curtis and Dad Eddie?

She pulled off the mask. "Boys, I'm going to be fine. Have you called your dads yet?"

He and Shane looked at each other and then back at their mother.

"Oh no. You thought they were inside." She shook her head. "They headed off to Denver this morning to get a car they bought."

Shane let out a big breath. "Thank God."

Relieved, Corey brought out his ROC. "You call Dads and Phoebe. I'll check with Nicole about Belle and Juan."

Before he could punch in the number, the alarm Jena had set up in the device went off.

Kip is inside the system.

* * * *

Belle ran out the back of the courthouse and saw Cindy holding a gun to Juan's head.

Chapter Fifteen

Bolting to the courthouse, Shane brought out his cell instead of the comprised ROC. Using the voice feature, he gave the command, "Call Belle."

Corey ran beside him.

Her voice mail came on, chilling him to his bones. *Where is she? Please, let Belle and Juan be safe.*

He and Corey came around the corner and saw a disastrous scene. "Where's Belle and Juan, Nicole?"

"Trollinger and Juan were gone when we got here. Belle got a text from Cindy and ran out the back."

From Cindy? That didn't make sense since Dylan still had Trollinger's cell. Where had she gotten a phone?

As they rushed to the door with their guns drawn, Corey yelled back at her. "Call Doc for help."

Before they got to the door, it opened and Juan ran inside into their arms.

Shaking, their boy blurted out. "She's got Mom."

Shane's gut tightened. *Trollinger.*

"They're gone." Juan's eyes welled up.

He shot out the door. Scanning the area, it was clear to him that Cindy must've gotten a cell from the bastard who had shot up the town and blown up his parents' business.

Kip's sister's car was nowhere to be found. There was no sign of the bitch or of Belle. Rushing back into the building, he saw Corey kneel down in front of Juan.

"Okay, son. Tell us exactly what happened."

"It was the lady in the room next to mine. When I heard the shooting in the hallway, I ducked down under my bed. Cindy came in, grabbed my legs, pulled me out, and put a gun to my head."

Where had she gotten a gun? Likely from the dead man in black. *I knew she couldn't be trusted.*

"She made me go outside to her car and kept telling me she was going to kill me if I didn't do what she said. Mom showed up. Cindy told Mom if she got in the trunk, I would be let go unharmed."

What do she and Kip want with Belle? It didn't make any sense.

"I didn't know what to do. I saw a rock and thought about throwing it at Cindy but she slammed down the lid on top of Mom before I had a chance to. Then she told me to close my eyes and count to one hundred or she was going to kill Mom."

All Shane could feel inside was pure rage.

Juan's eyes were wide. "As soon as I heard her drive off with Mom and thought she could no longer see me, I stopped counting and ran in."

That likely meant Trollinger had only a few seconds lead on them. The boat and the explosion had been a diversion to spread the team thin. *No one is guarding the bridge.*

"Did I do the right thing?"

"You did great." Corey pointed to Nicole. "Juan, stay here with Miss Nicole. We will go get Mom."

Shane ran around the courthouse with Corey. He brought out his cell. "Call Black."

As they sprinted, Corey pulled out the keys to his truck, which was parked out front.

"Shane, what's your status?"

Jumping into the passenger's seat of the truck, he filled Easton in on all that had gone down at the courthouse as Corey hit the gas. When they turned left on West Street, he saw Trollinger's car. "We've got eyes on her vehicle now, sir."

"We're on our way." By Black's heavy breathing, Shane knew he was running. "I'll get Jason on the horn with the state patrol. Keep the line open."

Setting up roadblocks would take too much time.

He and Corey had to catch the bitch. They had to save Belle.

Corey turned right without slowing down, causing the tires to squeal.

"We're half a mile from the bridge, sir." Shane was one of the best shots that came out of the Agency, but he wouldn't dare try until he knew he had a clean shot. Belle was in the trunk. "We are closing the distance."

The car ahead went over the bridge.

Shooting Trollinger or the tires was a risk at this high speed. But they didn't have a choice if they had any chance of saving Belle.

He aimed his gun, tightened his finger on the trigger. And then everything went to hell. The Silver Spoon Bridge blew up right in front of them.

Corey hit the brakes, bringing the truck to a stop just at the edge of the new drop-off the explosion had created.

Cursing, Shane slammed his fists into the dashboard. He'd failed Belle. She was gone, in the car of a madman's sister.

* * * *

Juan is safe.

No matter what happened—that was the most important thing to Belle.

But she wasn't ready to die. She had Juan, who needed her. She'd just found the loves of her life—Shane and Corey. *My family.*

Amber was going to have a baby. Belle was going to be an aunt. The orphans at the Boys Ranch needed her.

She had so much to live for.

Something had exploded just as they'd left Destiny. By the sound, she guessed whatever had suffered the bomb had to be near—the bridge or one of the buildings close to it.

Once again, she prayed for the sweet people of the town she loved. Paris, with her brilliant mind and warm heart. Gretchen and Ethel, the sweet matriarchs of Destiny. Kaylyn, whose love of animals and generous soul amazed everyone. And so many more. Every neighbor and shopkeeper, every teacher and student, every man and woman. Destiny was Belle's home.

Lunceford and his horrible sister had declared war on the town she loved, and right now, Belle was the only one on the front lines. What did Cindy want with her? Was she only a pawn in a much bigger evil scheme of Lunceford? She had no clue but knew she must fight. She wasn't going to give up until she drew her last breath. Nothing would stop her.

For the past couple of hours she'd been Trollinger's prisoner. The bitch had thrown Belle's cell to the pavement before shoving her into the trunk, leaving her no way to communicate.

Cindy's car was quite old, so there was no trunk release and the backseat didn't fold down. In the blackness, Belle had felt around for any tire-changing tools that could help her but found none. The only success she'd had was pulling out the wires from the brake lights. When she tried to push them out so she could stick her hand through to signal to others, neither one would budge. Her only hope was that a patrolman would see Trollinger's brake lights were out.

Now, all she could do was wait and pray.

* * * *

Corey drove the brand new Boys Ranch bus, whose passengers were the rest of Shannon's Elite—not counting Jena, Nicole, Cooper, and Jonas.

Jena had not only knocked Lunceford out of the system and off their ROC devices, but had also isolated the remote server farm where all his transmissions were originating. Kip's digital eyes, ears, and mouth were offline because of her. Jena remained at TBK and was still trying to lock on to the physical location of his data center.

Nicole had remained with the two fallen teammates.

They'd learned from a call from Doc that Cooper would survive, but Jonas was dead.

Corey's gut coiled into a knot of rage.

They'd lost so much time after the bridge exploded. Crawling down the ravine to the water below and swimming to the other side had slowed them down.

The Stone brothers had brought the bus down from the ranch, which was on the opposite side of the destroyed bridge. Their wife, Belle's sister, had been scared to death and made him and Shane swear they would save Belle.

That was exactly what he intended to do. *What I must do.* His pulse pounded like a jackhammer in his temples.

Black and Jason were in constant touch with local Wyoming law enforcement, trying to tighten the noose around Trollinger. Unfortunately, due to the unprecedented visit of the vice president to Cheyenne, the team only had access to a lone sheriff and two deputies. Black had been the one to say what they all already suspected. Lunceford had clearly chosen well his day of attack on Destiny.

Shane stared at the GPS. He was tracking the car that was taking Belle to some unknown destination. "Trollinger just took a right off of 287 onto Wyoming 135. About an hour ahead."

An hour too much.

* * * *

Belle heard a siren. *Please, God.*

Trollinger's car came to a stop.

The siren stopped.

Even her breathing stopped.

In that instant, everything came to a standstill in the deafening silence.

Belle screamed as loud as she could and kicked the lid of the trunk.

She heard gunshots.

The trunk opened.

Kip's sister glared at her, holding a gun. "Sit up, bitch."

She held her hands above her head. "Relax, Cindy." Out of the corner of her eye, she saw they were on a road that looked deserted other than the patrol car behind them.

"Don't you fucking tell me what to do. I'm the one in charge. Take a look at what you made me do."

The car's lights were still flashing, and the officer was on the ground bleeding.

"Let me go to him, Cindy." She could see the man was still breathing. "I can help."

"Fucking do-gooder." The woman walked over to the poor man and shot two more bullets into his head.

Belle's heart stopped.

"Try that again, Belle, and I'll put a bullet between your eyes. Am I clear?"

* * * *

Shane watched the dot on the screen start to move again, and his jaw clenched. Trollinger was getting away.

The deputy who had spotted the vehicle ten minutes ago, according to Sheriff Rose, his superior, had yet to radio back in.

Shane suspected the worst. *Please let Belle be okay.*

Jason had Rose on his cell's speaker. The sheriff was driving to the spot where Deputy Clarkson had reported pulling Trollinger over. Rose was three miles from the location. Corey kept closing the gap, but they were still at least forty-five minutes away.

Everyone in the van sat in silence, anxious to hear what the sheriff would find.

"I see flashing lights up ahead," Rose informed. "That's got to be Clarkson's car."

They all held their breaths.

"Oh my God. Clarkson's on the ground. He's been shot in the head. My deputy is dead."

Fuck.

Shane's blood turned icy in his veins.

"Now, it's personal." Rose's voice shook with rage. "There's no sign of the vehicle. I'm going to find that bitch."

Black took the cell and brought it up to his mouth. "Do not go by yourself, Sheriff. Wait for us. She won't be alone. This is an order."

"You can't give me an order, Agent Black. CIA has no jurisdiction on domestic soil. I'm the law in Freemont County."

"Marshal." Black held the phone up to Corey.

Shane looked over at his brother, whose face stormed with torment.

"Sheriff, this is U.S. Marshal Corey Blue. I *do* have jurisdiction. You will wait for our arrival. You will not go alone. Am I clear?" Corey was dying inside, just like Shane.

There was a pause. Finally, Rose said, "Get your asses here fast, Marshal."

"We will."

Trollinger was a murderer, just like her motherfucking brother. She had Belle and might be taking her to Lunceford. The bastard had orchestrated everything.

Trollinger showing up at Lucy's Burgers and feigning to pass out had been the beginning of it all. Why there? A place Belle just happened to be?

Kip had scripted Trollinger's role, including the part where she feared he was coming for her. But the maniac certainly didn't believe they would ever fully trust her. The reason for the coordinated attacks.

The explosives in the boat on Lover's Beach had just been a diversion to spread the team thin.

Blue's Diner blowing up was just another distraction, which forced him and Corey away from Belle.

Jena had uncovered the identity of the man in black who had showed up at the courthouse, injuring Cooper and killing Jonas. She'd uploaded her findings to all their ROCs. The shooter was a highly paid Russian assassin who specialized in bombs. Clearly, he was the one who had made the footprints in the snow, who had planted all the bombs around town, who had traveled to town by the boat they'd found on Lover's Beach.

Had Lunceford's intention been to get his assassin and Cooper and Jonas, two well-trained agents, to collide in a sea of bullets? Probably.

In all the confusion, Cindy had been able to force Juan out back to her car until Belle, who the bitch clearly knew would turn herself over for his release, had appeared.

The last explosion that took out the bridge, the only way in and out of Destiny by car, had been another piece of the puzzle.

From beginning to end, all of it—the bombings, the shootings, the kidnapping of Belle—was part of Lunceford's diabolical war on Destiny.

One question kept rolling around and around in Shane's head.

Why Belle? Why does Lunceford want her?

Chapter Sixteen

Belle felt Trollinger's car come to a stop and her hear skipped several beats.

What is Cindy going to do with me?

She hadn't been able to stop shaking since seeing the officer being shot in cold blood by the psychopath.

The trunk opened.

"Get out, bitch." Trollinger seemed to be in some kind of panic.

Why?

Cindy stood next to the car, but her captor wasn't alone.

Two large, scary-looking men flanked Kip's sister.

Belle climbed out. Her leg muscles were stiff from being cramped during the long ride.

The land was quite flat. This definitely wasn't Colorado.

As the sun dipped below the horizon, she could see the area was quite remote.

They were parked in front of a nondescript-looking building.

To her left were a couple of black sedans. To her right was a helicopter.

Is Kip inside?

Trollinger holstered her gun, which surprised Belle though it was clear the woman was still in charge. Cindy had the two men by her side. There were also three heavily armed goons on the rooftop that Belle had noticed. Who knew how many more were in the building?

"Belle, welcome to location zero-zero-seven."

She didn't miss the reference to James Bond. *More of Lunceford's arrogance, no doubt.*

"Why did you bring me here?"

"For my brother, of course." Cindy turned to the two thugs. "Get her into the building." The woman didn't wait to see if her orders were followed, but instead marched off to the entrance.

The one whose arms were covered in tats glared at her. "You heard the lady, *vozlyublennaya*."

Russian mobsters.

Belle was aware of what had happened to Phoebe in Chicago. It was well known that Mitrofanov's son Anton had betrayed his father. Anton was obviously still working with Lunceford.

Walking between the two men, Belle's thoughts were of Shane and Corey. In her heart, she had no doubt they—at this very moment—were using every means at their disposal to try to find her. Her guys were not the kind of men who gave up. But even with Black's help, how could Shane and Corey discover this remote place?

Somehow, she had to find a way to escape this nightmare.

I wish I knew how to fly a helicopter.

Of course, she didn't.

Her only hope was to get the keys to one of the cars, break free of Cindy and her thugs, and drive like hell out of here.

It was a long shot, but the only one she had left.

The two mobsters walked her down a hallway and through a set of doors. Cindy stood in front of a monitor and keyboard. The room was set up with the latest high-tech medical equipment.

It's an operating room. Maybe Kip actually did have leukemia. *Is that why Cindy brought me here?*

"I'm a nurse, but I can't perform a bone marrow transplant. You need a doctor for that. Someone who specializes in that kind of procedure."

The lunatic shoved Belle a good ten feet away by the surgical table. "You are not performing the procedure, you idiot. You are the donor."

Belle couldn't wrap her head around what she'd just been told. "That's impossible. I can't be a match for Lunceford."

"Yes, it's possible. By now you realize you cannot escape. I have ten heavily armed men here under my command that will ensure you stay put." Cindy placed her gun on the counter and began typing furiously on the keyboard, staring up at its monitor.

A man in scrubs walked into the room.

Cindy looked over her shoulder at her, a horrific, twisted grin spreading across her face. "Doctor." She turned to the two mobsters. "This bitch isn't going anywhere. Go check with Zakhar. See if he's heard from Kip. He should've been here by now."

The two men nodded and left.

"This has to be a mistake, Cindy. You're Lunceford's sister. The odds are you would be a match. Have you been tested?"

"Of course I was tested, bitch, but Kip and I are only half siblings. I would give my life for him, but it turns out that you will be the one to do that instead of me."

"Wait. I don't have to give my life. This is a simple procedure." Belle still didn't like the idea of anything from her body saving that monster. "Cindy, donating bone marrow doesn't end the life of the donor."

"Shut the fuck up. Of course I know that. But this is a special circumstance, and my brilliant brother doesn't ever leave loose ends. You are the perfect match, bitch."

Belle's head was spinning and her heart was racing. She spotted the table with the surgical implements. They were two steps to her left. The doctor was reading a chart, likely Kips.

I need to keep her talking. If I can just get my hands on one of those scalpels... "Was anything you told us true?"

"Some. Kip is my half brother. He changed my identity after he executed our father and his mother. He'd rescued me from a foster home when I was a teenager. He helped me find my mother. The bitch abandoned me when I was five years old." Cindy's voice became lyrical. "She had to die. She was my first."

Belle gulped, realizing what *first* must mean.

"Seeing the horror in her eyes when I put the knife to her throat was such a pleasure. Nothing like losing your virginity, is there?"

She's completely insane. Belle took a deep breath. *Insane or not, keep her talking. Sooner or later, they must intend to kill me.* "How can you be sure I'm a match?" She started to take a step to the instrument table, but the doctor suddenly glanced up from the chart.

She froze, praying for him to look down again.

"Not that it matters one way or the other whether you know or not, but you certainly must realize my brother is a genius. Kip hacked into the national bone marrow registry and found you and two other matches, but of course he chose you."

Belle had signed up with the national bone marrow registry when she'd worked in her ex's practice.

Ninety-three percent of patients were able to find one or two matches from the ten million plus potential registered donors. Kip found three.

Why do evil people like Lunceford always seem to be able to cheat the odds?

The doctor's eyes lowered back to the chart.

Cindy typed away on the keyboard, obviously still troubled about something. "I'm sure you know the reason he chose you over the other two, Belle."

"Because I'm from the town he's at war with." Belle inched quietly closer to the table of instruments.

"For an idiot, you're not as dumb as you seem." Cindy's tone had a noticeable edge of frustration. "Where is he?"

Kip isn't here.

She didn't bother looking at Belle, her attention glued to the monitor.

Obviously, the lunatic feels secure that I won't try to escape.

Belle held her breath, keeping her eyes on Cindy and the doctor.

Just a little closer...

A face she'd only seen in a picture on the cover of *Destiny Daily* appeared on the monitor.

Kip Lunceford!

The doctor looked up from the charts.

"Kip, where are you?" The relief in Cindy's voice was obvious.

Oh God, I have to escape. I have to survive this. I have to live. For Juan. For Shane and Corey. Even for me.

The murdering bastard's face was tight with frustration. "Get out now. I didn't plan for Shannon's Elite placing a tracker on your car, Cindy."

"Why didn't you contact me, brother?"

"Their fucking hacker was able to lock down my access. I wasn't able to send a message until now. They are less than five minutes away. Take the helicopter and bring Belle and the doctor to me at the secondary location."

The screen went dark.

It's now or never.

The surgeon nodded and reached for Belle.

Belle kicked the bastard as hard as she could in the nuts.

He doubled over, groaning.

In a split second, she grabbed a scalpel and leapt to Cindy, who was reaching for her gun.

Belle stabbed her in the hand, and the weapon slid off the counter onto the floor several feet away from them and the door.

Cindy ran out and screamed, "Grab the bitch and bring her to the helicopter."

The two thugs rushed in, their guns aimed at Belle.

She could hear the helicopter's engine revving up.

I've come too far to give up now.

An image of Juan standing between Shane and Corey filled her mind and gave her renewed courage.

If today is the day I must die, I won't go down without a fight.

Gunshots could be heard just outside the building.

The two mobsters turned to the door.

Keeping hold of the scalpel, Belle leapt for Cindy's gun.

"Bitch."

The other one shouted something in Russian.

Just as her fingers touched the gun, two shots rang out inside the room.

Had she jumped too late for Cindy's weapon?

She heard two heavy thuds behind her and then Shane and Corey saying her name.

"Belle."

She turned and saw the two loves of her life running to her side.

They wrapped her up in their arms and she felt tears of relief and joy fall from her eyes.

"You're here. You're really here."

Shane and Corey hadn't given up. They'd done the impossible. They'd saved her, and all the fear she'd been carrying since being shoved in the trunk vanished.

Shane's gaze was filled with love and concern. "Are you okay, baby?"

She nodded. "Is Juan okay?"

"He's with Amber. He's fine."

She closed her eyes, feeling completely relieved that her boy was in good hands.

Corey pressed his lips to hers. "It's all over, sweetheart."

Shane squeezed her hand. "We have you, and you're safe now."

Chapter Seventeen

Sitting at the local diner in Riverton, Shane held Belle's hand and his brother kept his arm around her shoulder. He and Corey had kept Belle between them ever since finding her at Kip's secret location. They'd lost her once. They would never let that happen again.

Black and Jason hadn't returned from finishing up the paperwork with Sheriff Rose at his office. Corey, as a US marshal, should've gone with them, too, but had refused, unwilling to leave Belle.

She looked around the table at the rest of the team. "I know I've said it already, but thank you all for everything. I can't express how grateful I am for what you did for me."

Jo smiled. "Just doing our job, Belle."

Shane knew it was more than just duty with the team. They cared about Destiny and cared about its citizens. He owed them. Without Shannon's Elite, the mission to save Belle would've failed.

Ten dead mobsters.

The team had proven themselves, though Kip was still missing and Cindy had escaped. They'd all gotten notified on their ROCs moments ago that the helicopter had been found abandoned in Idaho. Like the rest of Shannon's Elite, Shane believed Kip and his sister must be hiding out somewhere in the Northwest.

The doctor was in custody, but so far, hadn't given them anything useful that would help them find the two fugitives.

Belle's bravery amazed all of them. Her account of how she'd never given up, always looking for some way to escape, made him fall even deeper in love with her. She was the best thing that had ever happened to him.

Knowing she was a bone marrow match for the son of a bitch didn't sit well with either him or Corey. The entire team would be assigned to protect Belle until the SOB and his crazy sister were captured. Black had contacted Langley about the other two matches in the registry. They would be protected as well.

The waitress brought their meals. "Two ham and cheese sandwiches with fries?"

"That's me," Matt answered.

"And me." Sean nodded.

"Rib-eye steak medium rare?"

Dylan turned his head to her, still wearing his sunglasses, though it was nighttime. "Thank you."

The waitress passed out the rest of the food, placing the cheeseburger in front of Belle.

"Looks delicious." She turned to him. "I'm starving."

"Me, too." His stomach growled, reminding him how long it had been since he'd eaten. "No wonder, baby. We didn't get to have our lunch at Phong's."

Everyone began devouring his or her meal, except Belle, whose face suddenly turned white.

"What's the matter, sweetheart?" Corey asked. "Something wrong with your food?"

She shook her head. "I took a whiff and got queasy. I guess I'm still shook up from all that has happened. That poor deputy." Her eyes welled up. "If I hadn't pulled the wires on the brake light, he might've—"

"Sweetheart, take a couple of sips of water and breathe." Knowing the trauma she'd endured, Shane wanted to help her through all the aftermath. "Deputy Clarkson didn't pull Cindy over for faulty brake lights, Belle. Even though it was smart thinking to try to escape, very smart, the entire state of Wyoming was on the lookout for her car."

"That helps, Shane. I'm feeling a little better now."

"Would you like something else, Belle?" Jo asked from across the table. "Maybe some soup?"

"This is fine. I think I'll eat a few bites and see how it goes. I might have to get a takeout box."

Jason, Black, and Sheriff Rose came into the restaurant.

"Excuse me." Belle pushed away from the table and stood up.

He and Corey did the same, staying next to her.

She walked up to Rose. "I'm so sorry about your deputy."

He choked out. "William died a hero, Miss White."

Tears streamed down her face.

Grief stricken, the old sheriff wrapped his arms around Belle.

"Is there anything I can do for his family, Sheriff?" Belle's capacity for caring continued to surprise him. It was boundless.

Rose wiped his eyes. "I'm his only family, Belle. He came here several years ago as a troubled kid trying to steal from our local grocery store. He was just hungry. I took him under my wing. When William was old enough, he became my deputy, and a damn good one he was."

Corey grabbed his glass of water and held it up. "To Deputy William Clarkson, a fallen hero."

The team raised their glasses and in unison, said. "Here. Here."

Rose smiled. "Thank you."

Black held out his hand to the man. "I'll come back for William's service, Sheriff."

Sheriff Rose took Black's hand and shook it.

"We all will," Jason said.

Brock, the newest member of the team nodded. "Absolutely."

They'd gotten word from Doc that Cooper was stable. The team had another memorial to attend back in Destiny. Jonas Ward. Thankfully, the tracker that Shane and Corey had placed on Trollinger's car had led them to Belle, but it hadn't saved Jonas or Clarkson.

The body count would continue to rise until Lunceford and his sister were captured.

* * * *

Belle looked out the windshield of Corey's truck. They were driving to the Boys Ranch and she was vibrating with anticipation to see Juan, little Jake, and the other children.

Corey drove, and Shane held her hand. Her heart was theirs. She adored them.

She would build a life with them, one full of joy and laughter. They were her champions who had brought her out of the depths of despair and hopelessness. Shane and Corey had saved her not just from Kip, but also from herself. Her doubts were gone, thanks to her wonderful, amazing men. They'd shown her that she, too, deserved to be loved and happy.

A smile crossed her face.

"What are you thinking about, baby?"

She leaned into him. "About you, Corey, and Juan and the wonderful life we will have together."

Corey turned left and drove the truck past the Boys Ranch's gate.

Up ahead, she saw Juan standing by little Jake. Doc had released Juan that morning.

God, they look just like brothers. Jake's biological parents had been killed when he was only two years old. Living in the poorest part of Chicago, they had been innocent victims, accidently shot through their window during a gun battle between rival gangs. According to Jake's caseworker's account at the time, he had been asleep in his bedroom which ended up saving his life. The sweet boy had been in foster care ever since. The Boys Ranch would be his first real home.

Has Jake already stolen my heart?

Juan and Jake started screaming and running to greet her. Amber and her three husbands came out of the building with the other boys.

"Look what Juan and Jake made for you, sweetheart." Corey pointed to the sign that hung on the new dormitory.

Her heart swelled as she read the sign.

Welcome home, Mom.

Corey parked the truck and Shane stepped out, holding the door for her.

"Mom. Mom." Juan wrapped his arms around her waist. "I'm so glad you're home."

Little Jake copied Juan, like kids do. He grabbed onto her leg. "Mommy. Mommy. You're home. You're home."

She kissed them both, knowing these were her boys and she could never let them go. She turned to Corey and Shane. *What will my men think of that?* They'd already told her that they were ready to adopt Juan. That was a big step. Adopting two?

Corey lifted Jake up into his arms. "I think it's time to take this cowboy on a dragon hunt, Shane. Do you agree?"

Shane put his arm around Juan. "Maybe we should ask his big brother. What do you think, Juan?"

"Yes, Dad. Please. Could it just be us men, you, me, Pop Corey, and Jake?" Juan turned to her. "Is that okay, Mom? We really need some male bonding time."

She smiled. What a smart boy. Clearly, Juan was several steps ahead of all of them.

"Of course it's okay, son." She grabbed his and Jake's hand.

"Really?" Jake's eyes were wider than she'd ever seen them before.

"Yes." She kissed him on the forehead. "But the next time I'm going with you. You know how much I love dragon hunting."

"And I love you, mommy."

"I love you, Jake." Tears welled up in her eyes as the rest of her welcome party surrounded her.

* * * *

Inside the dormitory, Shane watched Belle tuck in the last of the little cowboys. He couldn't get over how lucky he was to have her.

Corey was walking around the property with the Stone brothers making sure no intruders lurked in the darkness. Precaution was the name of the game until Lunceford and his sister were captured.

Jaris sat next to Shane with Sugar, his German shepherd, at their feet. "Long day for these little guys."

"Yes it has been. Everyone is thrilled that you and Chance have agreed to be dorm supervisors at the Boys Ranch. You and Chance have been lifesavers staying here with the boys."

"We were restless. After I finished my training with Chance, we were already in talks with Kaylyn about coming to work for her to help train guide dogs." Jaris leaned down and petted Sugar. "Though I think the dogs train us, if the truth be known. Chance and I needed a place to stay and what better place than with these young men. So when the opportunity knocked, we came running. We're the lucky ones. Not only do we have a place to stay, but we also have the boys to help with the dogs. Kaylyn is really excited about the new training. It's great to be in partnership with her on this endeavor."

Shane sensed something in Jaris's tone that told him it was more than just a partnership to Jaris. The man clearly felt more for Kaylyn than just a business associate. "Sounds like you and Chance have grown quite close, Jaris."

Jaris nodded. "He's my brother. Losing my sight was tough. Not being a cop was even harder. He helped me through so much."

"Ditto, buddy." Chance walked over to them with Annie. "I had no idea I was black until you told me."

They all laughed.

Jaris shook his head. "How would I know if you are black or not, Chance? I was blind when I met you."

"Ah, that's right. I'm the one who told you. Since the boys are all tucked in, we better get to familiarizing ourselves with the building, Jaris."

Jaris stood up. "Shane, I'm still new to being sightless. Chance may have signed off on my training, but he will make sure I count every step in this place. I'm Luke Skywalker to his Yoda. By New Year's, I'll know every nook and cranny of this place. The boys won't be able to pull the wool over our eyes, so to speak."

Corey walked in. "Hey, fellas."

"Hi, Corey," Jaris said. "I'm looking forward to going dragon hunting with you guys sometime."

Chance nodded. "Me and Annie, too."

"Definitely, though I think we'll take out on foot instead of horseback."

"Hey, are you saying blind guys can't be cowboys? Dems fightin' words, Mr. Blue." Chance laughed.

Corey slapped the guy on the back. "I was thinking about Annie, Chance."

"We'll make sure the boys get a good night's sleep." Jaris headed to the door.

"Talk to you later." Chance followed him out.

Belle came over to him just as the two guys left. "Hey." She held her finger up to her lips and pointed to the sleeping boys behind her.

The three of them walked quietly into the hallway together.

"Hey, baby." Corey pulled her in tight. "Sorry if I'm dirty."

Shane had never seen his brother so happy before.

She smiled. "It's okay. It was great seeing you show the kids how to handle horses. You're both good with the boys and with animals."

"And with you, baby." Shane loved seeing the little blush of pink appear on her cheeks. "I think we could all use a shower."

"You ready to go, baby?" Corey asked her.

She frowned. "I hate leaving our boys."

Shane grabbed her hand. "Jake and Juan will be fine, baby."

"We'll stay at the house in town. That way, we can get up early and go meet with Ethel about the adoption." Corey turned to him and looked him straight in the eyes.

Shane knew exactly what he was thinking, though they hadn't talked about it. "We need to get Ethel up to speed that there's been a change in plans."

"Yes, we do," Corey chimed in.

Her eyebrows shot up. "What change? You're not getting cold feet are you? You still want to adopt Juan?"

Shane leaned forward. "Of course, we want to adopt Juan. He's our son. But we also want to adopt Jake."

"Yes, we do, bro." Corey stroked her hair. "Being a judge, she'll know what we need to do to expedite the process."

"Oh my God. Seriously? Do you really mean it? I love Jake so much. He and Juan are so close. Did you notice how much they look alike? You're not joking? Really? We're going to talk to Ethel about it tomorrow?"

He and Corey laughed.

"Baby, it's real." Shane couldn't wait to tell everyone that he was a dad to two wonderful boys. "We love Jake, too."

"He's our son, sweetheart." Corey touched her cheek. "Just like Juan."

"Oh my God." Belle kissed them both, back and forth. "I'm so happy. I doubt I will be able to sleep tonight."

Shane thought about stripping her out of her clothes right then and there. God, he wanted her so badly. "I think we can help you with that, though you won't be going to sleep right away. Let's go home."

* * * *

"It feels good to be home." Corey leaned back in his chair. "Especially with Belle."

Shane nodded. "It took you about ten minutes to shower and me about the same. How long has she been in the bathtub?"

His brother's impatience echoed his own. "She's a woman. They take longer. We have to be patient."

Shane looked at the time on his cell. "I wonder if she fell asleep."

He smiled. "I doubt that, though I wouldn't be surprised."

His brother became quite serious. "Should we ask her tonight, Corey?"

He knew what Shane meant. "Let's stick to the plan, bro. We've rehearsed our words. Lover's Beach. Tomorrow night. It will be Christmas Eve. I'm as anxious as you but it's got to be the right time, okay?"

"I know." Shane nodded. "She's ours. She will always be ours. I just am ready to make it official." He looked at his cell again. "It's been an hour. Time's up. You with me?"

"Damn right, I'm with you."

They both jumped to their feet, heading to the woman of their dreams, the woman they meant to spend the rest of their lives with.

* * * *

Belle stepped out of the tub and grabbed a towel, when the door opened.

Shane and Corey bolted into the bathroom. They were shiny clean, wearing nothing but shorts.

"Guys, is everything okay?"

They both smiled.

Shane grabbed her hand and let his eyes roam over her naked body freely. "Everything is perfect."

Corey took the towel from her and tossed it to the side. "I'll say."

She giggled, loving how they looked at her. "I'm still wet."

"And you're about to get even wetter." Shane lifted her up into his arms, looking like a man dying of thirst. "We are going to drown you in pleasure, baby."

She tingled from head to toe, feeling his hard muscles against her skin. She turned to Corey and smiled. "No fair. Two against one."

"No fair at all, sweetheart. We never play fair." Corey pressed his lips to hers, the kiss melting her and causing every cell inside her to erupt with desire.

He broke the kiss, and she buried her head into Shane's chest.

They took her to the bedroom.

Shane lowered her to her feet. He stepped back. "I just want to look at you, baby. Turn around slowly."

Corey grinned wickedly. "Now you're talking, bro."

As she turned around, goose bumps rose on her skin, realizing Shane and Corey enjoyed what they saw.

"My God, she's perfect from head to toe." Shane's awe-filled tone thrilled her.

Corey clicked on soft, romantic music.

Feeling their adoration and love overwhelmed her, and she floated on the harmonies of the sexy song. Washed in sensuality, she let her hands roam over her body to the rhythm of the music.

Shane's eyes were hot with desire. "Oh my God. I've never seen anything more beautiful."

"Absolutely gorgeous." Corey's words rumbled deep in his chest.

Watching them, she sensed they were on the edge of their control. She enjoyed the impact her dance was having on them. How long could they hold back their lust before they ravished her into dreamy oblivion? She glanced down at their shorts, which could barely contain their hardening cocks.

Slowly and sensually, she licked her lips, hoping to excite them even more.

It clearly worked, as their breathing became hot and labored.

"Damn, bro. I can't take much more of this." Corey's confession spurred her on more.

She brought her hands up to her breasts and squeezed them, looking at him seductively.

Shane blew out a lungful of air. "Holy hell. I'm burning up for her."

Slowly vibrating to the music, she moved close to them, placing her fingertips on their muscled chests. She glided her hands down to the tops of their shorts and quickly unbuttoned each of them, one at a time.

Kneeling on the floor, she pulled their shorts down to their feet. Grabbing their huge erections, she kissed each one back and forth.

"Our baby has a naughty streak, doesn't she?" Shane looked at her with eyes full of desire.

Corey nodded, his face tight with hunger. "I love her style, bro, even if she's pushing me to the brink."

Shane grabbed her by the back of the head. "Time to turn the tables on our baby, don't you think? Show her what we're capable of."

"Hell yeah. Past time." Corey pulled her off the floor and into his arms. "Guess who is in charge, sweetheart?"

"You are. You and Shane."

He lowered her to the bed and crawled on top of her, pinning her body with his muscled frame.

Seducing them had been fun. Now she was face to face, body-to-body with their dominance and loving every bit of it.

Shane moved onto the bed. Corey pulled her onto her side, facing him, placing her between him and Shane. *This is where I belong.*

They held her for a moment, clearly trying to gather their will. She grinned, pleased that she'd had such a powerful impact on her guys.

Corey devoured her lips, increasing her desires. She'd never wanted anyone as much as she did Corey and Shane now. Her need to be filled by them, consumed and possessed by them, was overpowering, swamping her very being. She was completely lost to her desires and the pressure rose inside her until her pussy ached.

She was so wet and on fire.

Corey leaned down and sucked on her breasts, and Shane massaged her ass with his hands. The combination put her body in flames, increasing her cravings for more. She reached down and grabbed Corey's cock. He groaned, which thrilled her. Shifting her ass backward against Shane's dick, she began rotating her hips.

Corey and Shane shifted down her body until their hot tongues bathed her flesh, Corey's on her pussy and Shane's on her ass. The intimacy made her temperature spike hot. Feeling the intensity of their love for her sent warmth through her body that reached into her heart.

Their double oral pleasure was driving her wild.

Shane applied lubricant to her anus, which sent a shiver up and down her spine. "I can't wait to be inside this pretty ass, baby."

Corey continued licking her swollen, wet folds, as Shane circled her tight ring with his thick fingers.

"Oh yes. Please." Her suffering was so great. She grabbed the back of Corey's head, trying to find any relief from the hot storm of desire in her body.

He pressed on her clit with his thumb and a quake shot through her.

"I can't take much more. Please. I have to have you inside me. Please. Oh, please."

Shane kissed the small of her back and began fingering her ass. "That's what I like to hear, Belle. Begging."

Her body shook with desire. Her pussy clenched and her clit and nipples throbbed together as if they were connected by some invisible line.

Corey looked up at her from between her legs. "The sweetest sound on earth."

The pressure was so intense, so powerful. Aware of the lifestyle they practiced, she pleaded, hoping they would have mercy on her. "Please make love to me. I'm yours. All of me."

As Corey shifted up her body, she could feel the tip of Shane's cock press against the entrance to her ass. She pushed back into him, taking in the tip of his dick into her ass.

"Damn, baby. You're on fire." Shane kissed the back of her head. "Let me see if I can help you." He thrust his cock deep into her body, stretching her wide.

She moaned as the sting and pleasure rocked her entire body.

Corey's hot gaze melted her as he slid his cock past her pussy's lips and into her channel.

"Oh God. Yes," she yelled as she felt the pressure of both their massive cocks filling her.

Their synchronized thrusts, one shoving in and one pulling out, increased the building pressure inside her to its breaking point.

Her pussy spasmed uncontrollably and she clenched down on Shane and Corey as her orgasm rolled through her in hot, shivering waves of sensations.

Her body tightened and she clenched her fists, writhing between her men.

"Fuuuck. Yes." Shane growled behind her, sending his throbbing cock deep into her ass and holding it there.

Corey pumped his dick into her pussy a few more times, before thrusting his dick all the way into her body.

As they sent their seed into her, she came with them, every cell erupting in a giant fiery explosion of release.

Remaining in their arms for several sweet, breathless moments, she felt the flutters of their lovemaking throughout her body begin to slowly subside until she completely relaxed. "I never dreamed I could be this happy."

"Baby, you're the dream." Shane said, kissing her neck. "You're my happiness. I'm so deeply in love with you."

"I love you, Shane."

Corey kissed her sweetly. "Sweetheart, you fulfill my every longing, my every hope, my deepest desires. You are mine and I am yours. I will love you for eternity."

"I love you, Corey. I love you both so very much." As much-needed sleep began to overtake her, she imagined the life she would have with them, a life full of joy.

* * * *

Belle sat between Shane and Corey in the judge's chambers in the Swanson County Courthouse. They explained to Ethel about wanting to adopt Jake as well as Juan.

"Adopting one child is a big step. Two? Well, that's quite the leap." Ethel looked at all three of them. "You're sure about this?"

Shane nodded. "Absolutely."

Corey grabbed Belle's hand and squeezed. "Positively, without a shadow of a doubt."

Ethel turned to her. "What about you, Belle? You ready to be the mother of these two boys?"

"With or without the legal papers, I already am their mom with all my heart."

"That's all I wanted to hear. I will have to talk to the boys, but I've seen how they are around the three of you. I'm pretty sure what they will say." Ethel opened her drawer and pulled out some paperwork. "Shane and Corey are from Destiny, so they are somewhat familiar with how this works. In the eyes of Colorado, Belle, you need to marry one of them. That will make the adoption process move much quicker."

"But I want them both to adopt the boys, Ethel, and I want to marry both of them."

"In the eyes of Destiny, you will be married to both. As far as the adoption, I've set up multiple guardianships quite a few times. Shane and Corey will be Juan and Jake's dads in the eyes of Destiny and in the eyes of the law. The sooner you get married the sooner we can start the adoption."

"Really?" Belle looked into Ethel's eyes.

Ethel nodded. "It's that easy. When do you plan on getting married?"

She shrugged. "They haven't asked me."

"We can fix that right now." Ethel gave Shane and Corey a stern look. "Down on your knees."

Without hesitation, Shane and Corey knelt down in front of Belle, each taking one of her hands.

Her heart accelerated to a breakneck speed. "Oh my God. Is this really happening?"

"Everyone in town knows how crazy these two are about you, honey." Ethel shook her head. "Well, gentlemen? Don't keep the lady waiting."

Shane squeezed her hand. "Belle, I knew the first time I saw you that you were going to change my life. You did. I'm a different man, a better man. Being with you, I see everything differently. You're beautiful inside and out. Whenever I look at you, I feel like I'm having a wonderful dream except my eyes are open."

Corey smiled up at her. "I've never known a person as tenderhearted and loving as you. You are my past, Belle. I was always searching for you. You are my today. I love being with you. You are my tomorrow, my future. I want to spend the rest of my life with you."

Shane brought out a tiny box from his pocket and held it up for her. Corey opened the lid and she saw the engagement ring with two interlocking bands with an emerald-cut diamond.

Corey's loving gaze melted her completely. "This was our grandmother's ring, Belle."

"The two bands represented her two husbands, our grandfathers. Now, they will represent Corey and me."

In unison they said, "Will you marry us, Belle White?"

With tears welling up in her eyes, she looked at her amazing, wonderful men. "You planned this, didn't you? This wasn't a spur of the moment thing, was it?"

Ethel wiped her eyes. "Belle, please. Answer them."

"Yes. Yes. I will marry you both. I love you so much."

They wrapped her up in their arms and showered her with kisses.

"That was beautiful." Ethel might run her court with an iron fist but she had the softest heart. "Any ideas when you want to have your wedding? I'm not rushing you, but like I said, the sooner the better for the adoption."

Shane's eyebrow shot up. "Sooner is good. Is it possible we could get it done today?"

"I like that idea, bro." Corey turned to Ethel. "Is it?"

Belle smiled. They were as anxious as she was to get married. "Guys, there's got to be a waiting period, right Ethel?"

"There is, but you're looking at a judge who can waive that. I have the power." Ethel opened her drawer again and pulled out more paperwork. "Just so happens I have a marriage license right here."

"How did you know?" Shane asked.

The dear woman winked. "Because I'm the judge, Shane Blue. I know everything. Well, Belle? You ready to make honest men out of these two hoodlums?"

"Who are you calling hoodlums, Ethel? I'm a US marshal and Shane is a CIA agent."

Belle laughed.

"Okay. Two legalized hoodlums. Don't forget, Corey Blue, I knew you when you went joyriding with your brother when you were only twelve, long before you had a driver's license."

"Yes, ma'am. I remember. You scared the daylights out of me when my parents brought me to court. I thought you were going to send me away for good."

Ethel laughed. "That's my job. Look at you now. I'm partially responsible for the wonderful man you've become. Now, back to the matter at hand. Belle, would you like to get married today, right now?"

"With all my heart, yes. But I want to call Amber. I'd like her to be one of my witnesses."

"Juan and Jake, too," Shane added, making her love him even more.

Corey nodded. "I think Mom, Dads, and Phoebe need to come, too."

"Call everyone." Ethel was all smiles. "The wedding is in an hour."

* * * *

Belle hugged Juan and Jake again.

Jake squeezed her leg. "I love you, Mommy. You look so pretty."

"I love you, too, little man."

Juan took her hand. "Mom, don't mess up your makeup again or Aunt Amber is going to be mad at me and Jake."

"I can't help it, boys. I'm just so happy." Ethel's chamber was packed with their witnesses. Belle grabbed Amber's hand. "Shane, Corey, and I would like to have another service at the ranch." She glanced down at Juan and Jake. "We just want to make it legal so we can adopt you boys sooner."

"I would love that, Sis."

Ethel took charge. "Everyone please gather around. Belle, you stand between Shane and Corey."

They took their places.

Ethel began the ceremony. "We are here because the three of you have decided to join your lives. You come here with precious gifts—mature understanding, your love, your hopes and dreams, your trust in one another, and your faith in life's meaning and purpose, resolved to share life's experiences in enduring love and loyalty. The decision has been made in your hearts and minds, and we are here to witness the public expression of the commitments you have made privately to each other. Marriage is a relationship not to be entered into lightly or thoughtlessly, but reverently, soberly, with deep purposes and in the spirit of enduring love. Much is required of you three. Knowing this, does each of you wish to proceed with this marriage?"

She and her grooms said "yes" in unison.

"Shane and Corey, will you take Belle as your wife? Will you love her, comfort her, honor and keep her in sickness and in health, in sorrow and in joy, and will you live for her, before all others, as long as you all shall live?"

"We will," they answered in unison, causing Belle's heart to swell with joy.

"Belle, will you take Shane and Corey as your husbands? Will you love them, comfort them, honor and keep them in sickness and in health, in sorrow and in joy, and will you live for them, before all others, as long as you all shall live?"

"I will."

"Please face each other, joining hands as a symbol of your union."

Shane and Corey each took one of her hands.

"Shane and Corey, will you then repeat after me? I, say your name, take you, Belle..."

As they repeated the rest of the vow, pledging their undying love to her, Belle knew her life had just begun.

"...so long as we shall live." Shane and Corey squeezed her hands again.

"Belle, will you then repeat after me?"

Every word sealed her to them forever. "I, Belle, take Shane and Corey to be my husbands. To live with you from this day forward. For better, for worse. In plenty and in want. In strength and in weakness. To love and to cherish. So long as we shall live."

Ethel nodded. "Shane, Corey, and Belle, having declared your vows in the presence of these witnesses and by the joining of hands, now therefore, by virtue of the authority vested in me by the state of Colorado, I do now declare in the presence of these gathered that you are husbands and wife. You may kiss the bride."

Corey and Shane kissed her. *They are my husbands and I am their wife.*

Everyone clapped.

"Mommy just got married to our daddies, Juan."

"Yes, she did, Jake."

Chapter Eighteen

Silver Spoon Bridge still had to be repaired from the explosion. According to all indications, the bridge wouldn't be navigable until sometime in June or July. The logistics about getting people and goods into Destiny had been quite an ordeal, but with the Golds and Knights on the job, everything had been worked out. Until the bridge was fully repaired, getting in and out of Destiny required travel via boats from the fishing dock on the other side of the lake to Lover's Beach. The boys didn't mind one bit.

Hearing them singing Jingle Bells at the top of their lungs made Shane laugh. He'd never seen such excitement in a group of kids in his life.

Landing at the beach, the boys marched to the two vans his dads had loaned to the Boys Ranch for transport in town.

Belle sat between him and Corey in the lead van.

Cody Stone directed the choir from the front seat, also singing quite loud. Bryant drove. Emmett and Amber were with the rest of the boys in the other van.

Belle leaned into him and whispered. "The boys are so excited about seeing Santa Claus and having a party."

"Yes they are." Shane looked over at Juan and Jake, their two sons. He was overcome with love for them. "Corey, I can't wait to see our boys' faces when Santa brings them their special present, can you?"

"I haven't been this excited about the O'Learys' Christmas party since I was a kid and we got our puppy."

"Me either."

Belle shook her head. "Stop it, you two. I'm dying of anticipation."

He and Corey had the best wife any two men could ask for in Belle. She was all he needed for the next hundred Christmases.

As the vans turned onto O'Leary Circle, Shane looked at all the cars parked up and down the street. Like every year, the entire town came to the O'Learys on Christmas Day. Destonians loved spending time together. Since these young men were the town's most special guests this year, parking spaces were reserved for their vans.

Bryant drove through the gates to the O'Learys' estate.

"Is that a real dragon, Juan?" Jake pointed out the window to the thirteen-foot tall bronze statue, the largest dragon depiction in town.

"No, but Mr. Patrick says it looks just like the dragon that rescued him back when he was in the Korean War."

"Wow. Is this Mr. Patrick's castle?"

Shane thought it was a fair question, since the O'Leary home looked gothic and was so massive.

"Yes, Jake," Juan answered. "It's his castle. His and Mr. Sam's and Miss Ethel's."

Though some of the boys had seen the O'Learys' home during the Halloween party, for the later arrivals to the ranch like Jake, this was their first time.

"Boys, remain in your seats until the van stops." Belle knew just what to say to get the kids to settle down. "I know you are excited, but safety first."

"Yes, ma'am," they said together.

Amber added, "And when we're inside, you need to be on your best behavior."

Again, they responded like little gentlemen with, "Yes, ma'am."

As the boys filed up to the door, their eyes were as wide as could be, taking in all the O'Learys' holiday decorations. They had the top-of-the-line animatronics fit for any theme park in the country. Elves popped out of boxes. Deer grazed on the snow-covered lawn. Angels flew down from hidden wires suspended from the trees.

He and Corey kept Belle between them. Protecting her was a lifelong joy, but they both would remain especially vigilant until Lunceford was captured or was dead.

The giant double doors opened and Ethel, dressed as Mrs. Santa as she was every year, greeted them. "Merry Christmas, boys. Come in. Come in. Everyone has been anxiously awaiting your arrival."

As they walked in, the boys noticed they all had stockings hanging from the banister. The smiles on their faces were priceless.

"You may grab your stockings as you come in, young men."

The boys' comments warmed all their hearts.

"I've never had a Christmas stocking."

"For me? Really."

"Mine is red. How did Santa know that was my favorite color?"

"There's candy and toys inside."

"This is the best Christmas ever."

Ethel smiled. "There's more, boys. Just you wait."

They followed her into the big ballroom. The boys' mouths were wide open in awe. Shane was having trouble keeping his from dropping.

Belle squeezed his hand. "Oh my God. This looks just like the North Pole."

"The O'Learys do this every year, baby."

Corey nodded. "Only they keep adding to the decorations. It gets more and more grand year after year. See." He pointed to the corner where the tree stood.

"It reaches to the ceiling. It's so beautiful."

Shane put his arm around her shoulder. "Every person in Destiny has an ornament on that tree."

"Even me, Daddy?" Jake walked up, holding his stocking, which was almost as big as him.

He leaned down and kissed him on the forehead. "Even you. At the New Year's party, we all get to take our ornaments home as a keepsake."

"Children, take a seat on the floor in front of Santa's throne. Adults, please gather round." Patrick, Ethel's dragon master husband, held a microphone. Unlike Halloween, Patrick was dressed like a giant elf, complete with pointy ears.

Belle hugged Jake. "Go join the other boys, honey. Sit with Juan."

Jake smiled and ran to his big brother.

He, Belle, and Corey sat down on one of the many sofas. Next to them were Doc and Mick. Paris sat several seats away. The three kept stealing glances at one another. When would they ever realize they were meant for each other?

Ethel stood next to Patrick. Music filled the room, announcing Santa's arrival.

This was Sam's day to be center stage.

Suddenly, the doors to the back lawn were opened and Father Christmas rode in on his red Harley Davidson.

Everyone cheered but the boys cheered the loudest.

Santa parked right in front of the children gathered on the floor. "Ho. Ho. Ho. Merry Christmas."

Ethel smiled. "Merry Christmas, Santa. We have a bunch of good boys and girls with us today."

"So I see, Mrs. Claus." Wearing the Santa suit, Sam walked up to his red throne.

As the O'Learys continued mesmerizing the children as they'd done to Shane since he was a kid, he smiled. Patrick and Sam adored Ethel. Shane saw in them the future he would spend with Belle and Corey.

The O'Learys handed out gifts to all the children. The boys from the ranch were clearly blown away by the wonderful presents Santa and Destiny had given them.

Belle beamed with pride. "Look at Juan helping Jake with his bike."

Corey smiled. "Jake will be able to ride without those training wheels in no time at all."

Shane gazed lovingly at their boys.

Belle grabbed his and Corey's hands. "The boys were right. This is the best Christmas ever."

"Damn right it is, sweetheart." Corey touched their wife's cheek. "Because you're here with us."

Damn right, indeed.

After all the gifts were passed out, his excitement exploded when he saw Santa, Mrs. Claus, and Patrick the elf walk over to Juan and Jake.

He leaned over to Belle and Corey. "It's time."

Tears welled in her eyes and a smile crossed Corey's face.

The Christmas trio walked their boys over to them.

Santa leaned down to Juan and Jake and said, "We have one last present for you."

"For me?" Jake clapped his hands together.

"Yes, Jake. For you and Juan." Sam smiled. "Take it away, Mrs. Claus."

Ethel got down to the boys' level, holding paperwork in her hand. "Boys, this present isn't from me or Santa. It's from your mommy and daddies. Remember when I talked with you about them? You told me how much you loved them."

Juan nodded, his eyes welling up just like Belle's.

"I do love them, Mrs. Santa." Jake's words melted all their hearts. "I love them very much."

A single tear ran down Ethel's cheek. "And they love you so very much, too." She turned to him, Belle, and Corey. "I would like to present to you Juan and Jake Blue."

Jake shook his head. "But my last name is Flores, Mrs. Santa."

"Not anymore, little brother." Juan wiped his eyes.

"Jake, you and Juan are officially brothers, and sons of Belle, Shane, and Corey. That's why your last name is Blue."

"Really? You can do that? Right now?"

"I'm a judge," Ethel said with a smile. "Yes. I can do that right now."

Jake turned to Belle. "Am I really yours, Mommy? For always?"

Belle pulled him and Jake into a hug. "Yes, baby. You and Juan are mine."

"And mine," Corey said. "For always."

"Now and forever." Shane had never felt such joy in all his life. "You are our sons."

He and Corey wrapped their arms around their family. *The best Christmas ever!*

* * * *

Belle walked out to the back lawn with the rest of the Christmas crowd. "A sleigh with real reindeer. I know I shouldn't be shocked, but all I can say is 'wow.'"

"Corey and I are going to help the Stone brothers line up the boys for the sleigh rides from Santa, but before we go, we want to ask you something."

She grinned. "We're already married, guys. You can't propose again."

Corey laughed. "If we did, I would expect another 'yes.'"

She kissed him lightly on the lips. "And you get one, too."

Shane grabbed her hand. "It's about where we're going to live."

Corey leaned over to her. "We talked with the Stones, and they would be happy to deed us a couple of acres to build a house on."

"We think Juan and Jake would like being close to the other boys." Shane smiled. "How would you like to live at the Boys Ranch?"

"Yes. Yes. Yes." She hugged them both. "I would love that."

Corey put his arm around her. "Tonight, we stay at our house in town with Juan and Jake. Shane and I wanted our little family together alone for one night."

Shane nodded. "After that, we'll move up to the ranch and stay in the spare apartment in the dormitory." The place had been built to accommodate double the number of boys that were currently living there, and there were two apartments inside for the dorm supervisors. "That way, Juan and Jake will have time to adjust to us and still continue to be with the boys."

Jaris and Chance lived in one of the apartments but the other one was vacant. The two men and their sweet guide dogs would make great neighbors.

"You two take such good care of me and our boys. I think it's a wonderful plan."

Shane looked pleased. "Good. That's settled."

Amber walked up to them carrying two steaming cups. "Hot chocolate, anyone?"

"I'd love some, Sis." She took one of the cups. The air was crisp but not too cold.

"None for me, Amber." Shane kissed Belle. "We better go help, Corey."

"You stay here, sweetheart, with your sister." Corey pressed his lips tenderly to hers.

Knowing how protective he and Shane were, she said, "I will."

Her two guys trotted off to help Santa.

Amber took a sip from her mug. "What a night, Belle."

"The best ever." Watching Shane and Corey hoist Juan and Jake up into the sleigh thrilled her. "I feel like my life is so complete, Sis, except one thing is missing." Belle knew Amber would understand. "Is that terrible to say?"

"Of course, not. After all you been through, you have a right to feel or say anything. Tell me what's bothering you."

"I love them so much, but they keep treating me like I'm made of porcelain. I'm not that fragile, Amber. I know they are members at Phase Four and I know that they are in the lifestyle. Why haven't they brought me there?"

"I'm sure they have their reasons, Sis. They are Doms. Take it from me, a woman who has three of her own. They'll come around. It really is a big step."

"Maybe so, but look at you. We share DNA. Can you imagine what I'm going through? I am desperate to experience Shane and Corey's life. All of it."

"Have you talked to them about how you're feeling?"

"No. I don't want them to think I don't enjoy our sex life because I do. Very much."

"You simply must be honest with them, Belle. True Doms would understand. If this is something you need to experience, that's what they need, too. That's what fulfills Doms, making sure their sub is totally fulfilled."

"When did you get so smart? You're the little sister, not me."

"You said it yourself, Belle. We share DNA."

Chapter Nineteen

Inside their apartment at the Boys Ranch, Corey studied the preliminary blueprints with Shane that Lucas had drawn up for the new house they were going to build for Belle and their boys. Lucas had done a rush job on it for them. He was a good friend.

"You know, our lovely wife's input is all over this design, Shane." He looked at all the colored sticky notes with her handwriting that dotted the pages, making it look a little like a patchwork quilt.

"I know. The kitchen is going to be twice the size from the original plan."

"And we've added two more bedrooms and another bathroom because she thought it best."

Corey laughed. "Actually, she designed this home as much as Lucas did."

They were going to start construction right after the New Year's party. He couldn't wait to begin.

Shane looked up from the blueprints. "Jake and Juan are adjusting beautifully, don't you agree, bro?"

"Yes, they are." Corey looked at the lines on the page that were going to give them each their own room in the house. He bet they would want to share a room for a few more years.

Belle came in, smiling. "May I show you two something on the computer?"

Shane nodded, coming to his feet.

"Sure, sweetheart." He pushed his chair back and stood.

They followed her into the other room. On the screen was Phase Four's website.

He looked at her and saw curiosity and excitement on her face.

Belle clicked on the information page about BDSM. "I find this intriguing."

Shane smiled. "You do?"

"Yes. Very. In fact, I've talked to Amber about it. I know you are members of the club and that you are in that lifestyle. I want to experience everything about you. Will you take me? I really want to go."

Shane turned to him. "What do you think? Is our baby ready?"

Corey bent down and brushed his lips to hers. "She's ready and so am I."

* * * *

Belle walked into Phase Four between her two fashion consultants for the evening. Shane and Corey had selected her outfit, which was the sexiest thing she'd ever seen and definitely the most revealing she'd ever worn. She felt somewhat shy, but also exhilarated and free. Her worst fear was falling, making a fool of herself in the black stilettos. *I can't believe how tall the heels are.* Since the leather skirt was so short and they'd refused to let her wear panties, if she fell, there would be nothing left to anyone's imagination.

Wouldn't that be quite the entrance for me? She stifled a nervous giggle.

That thought, to her surprise, was very exciting.

The skimpy silky top felt good on her skin, though so sheer it was nearly see-through.

She was vibrating from head to toe with excitement. Thank God, her two guys had agreed to take her to the club after she'd shown them the Phase Four website page she'd been scanning. She'd been waiting for her introduction into the life for some time, and now it was finally here—*with them. My guys.*

The place was packed.

Mr. Gold, the owner of the place, sat behind the desk in the outer room where members passed through to get to the play areas of Phase Four. "Welcome, Belle. I've got all the paperwork ready for you. Shane and Corey told me you were coming."

Her two men were in charge of everything, and she was more than happy about that. "Thanks, Mr. Gold."

His daughter Rylie had been one of the girls who had helped bake the apple pies.

"Please call me Zac."

"Sure thing." *Oops.*

She remembered Shane and Corey's instructions to her. Once inside the club, no talking to anyone unless they gave their approval. She looked over at her two Doms, hoping they would forgive her tiny mistake. Were they oblivious of her infraction?

Zac handed her the consent forms and a pen. "Is it still snowing?"

She bit back her response and stole another glance at Shane and Corey.

They both gave her a nod.

She felt her shoulders relax. "It's really coming down."

Her guys clearly hadn't been oblivious when she'd spoken without their approval. Would she be punished because of it? Wasn't the structure of this lifestyle one that appealed to her? Outside these walls, this life, things weren't always black and white.

"I bet we have snow on the ground until April." Corey put his arm around her, pulling her in tight.

She knew he loved her, but believed his current hold was also his way of demonstrating his possession of her. Not a problem, since she couldn't get enough of his touch.

"Snow until April, you say?" Gold asked. "The O'Learys will be happy about that, especially Sam. I'm sure he'd love to give sleigh rides in Santa's sled for the kids until Easter if he could."

"No doubt about that, Gold." Shane took the form she'd signed and inked his name above hers.

Corey followed suit. "It's official. We can take our sub inside."

Our sub. God, I love the sound of that.

"You're all set up, fellas."

"Which stage is ours, Gold?" Corey asked.

"Stage two. I'm sure you're going to give quite the show. Enjoy."

Her heart seized in her chest. *Stage two?* Were they going to put her on display her first night at the club? She told herself to breathe, but that was easier said than done. According to her sister, her guys didn't put Amber on display for their first several trips to the club. Did Shane and Corey mean to break Belle into the big league her very first night at Phase Four? Anxiety cramped her stomach.

Just put one stiletto in front of the other, Belle.

Shane and Corey led her through the door. The space was bigger than it looked from the outside. She'd driven by it a hundred times, but her dreams of the place paled in comparison to the reality.

Phase Four reminded her in part of the theatrical playhouses she'd attended back in Chicago. The sides of the large, expansive room had stages for the actors, Doms and subs. Chairs for the patrons, members in the life to watch. The other part of the space was like a giant nightclub. In the center of Phase Four was a dance floor, filled with couples, triples, and even quads gyrating sensually to the beat of the rhythmic music. Sofas in little alcoves held lovers who kissed, touched, and fondled each other without even the hint of shame.

She gasped, seeing two men paddling a naked woman on one of the platforms with about twenty members watching. The whole scene wreaked havoc with her insides. Her heart skipped several beats. Her breathing became shallow. Her pulse burned hot in her veins. Imagining what it would feel like to be in the woman's position, she was both turned on and jittery at the same time.

"Our stage is over here, sub." Shane led her to the platform.

She thought about calling out the word that would bring her two Doms to a screeching stop.

Freeze.

So simple really. Like the children's game, only without touch. *My safe word.* She had other words, also temperature related that were to be used to communicate her state. "Chilly" meant they were pushing her to a line she wasn't ready to cross. "Warm" told them she liked what they were doing. And so on.

Shane jumped up on the platform and held out his hands to her.

Corey grabbed her by the waist. "Breathe, baby."

"Yes, Master," she responded as they'd instructed her to do.

He lifted her up and Shane grabbed her. With her feet on the stage, she looked up into Shane's eyes.

"Damn, you are beautiful."

She glanced at the items on the platform. There was an odd-looking table, which she could see was adjustable. It looked as if it could be raised, lowered and tilted easily. Attached to it on all sides were leather restraints for wrists and ankles. There were shelves near the table that were filled with every sex toy imaginable and some unimaginable. Vibrators, paddles, whips, ropes, and so many things she didn't even recognize. A shiver ran up and down her spine.

Corey came up behind her and placed his hands on her shoulders. "Time to turn around and take a really good look at Phase Four, sub."

He spun her around, remaining behind her.

With her eyes wide open, she took it all in. Even only being up a few feet from the main floor, the stage gave her a better view. She guessed the crowd to be close to one hundred, which seemed like a lot, since Destiny was a small town. But she shouldn't be surprised since so many residents were members of the club. Thankfully, she only saw a few that she knew well. Paris stood in the corner talking with Jennifer Steele. Neither seemed to notice her or anyone else for that matter.

Corey reached around her and cupped her breasts. A few faces turned her direction and suddenly she couldn't breathe.

Shane stepped beside her and in his hand was a paddle. "What state are you in?"

How do I answer him?

She'd been a nurse for several years. Her adrenal medulla was in overdrive, pumping more and more of the hormone into her veins. Her training told her that her shallow respiration, elevated temperature and rapid heartbeat were due to the adrenaline coursing through her bloodstream.

Shane moved right in front of her, blocking her view of the rest of the club. She looked up at him and saw in his eyes love and concern. She was safe with him and Corey. Always.

"Sub, I asked you a question. Answer me." His eyes might've had softness but his tone definitely held an edge of frustration.

"Warm, Master. I'm warm."

"Tell us more, baby." Corey remained behind her, reaching under her top. He massaged her breasts through the lacy bra they'd also bought her.

"I'm nervous, Sir. Being up on this stage…wasn't something…I…uh…expected."

Shane grinned. "Absolutely perfect." He looked past her to Corey, who remained behind her. "We were right, bro."

"Yes, we were."

Right about what? About me?

Shane unbuttoned her top. "You are mine and Corey's, Belle."

Corey's lips feathered against her ear, causing her skin to tingle. "We want to show you off to everyone, sweetheart."

Their words and touches lit her up like flames to gasoline. She was their wife, their sub, their everything. No matter what happened, that would never change. They'd proven to her again and again how much they loved her.

"Let's get our baby more comfortable, Corey." Shane removed her top, and for the first time in her life she was in a public place with only her bra on.

Even though Shane remained in front of her, out of the corner of her eye she saw a few members taking seats right in front of their stage.

They are all less than four feet away. Oh my God.

Telling herself that the bra covered as much as any of her bikini tops, she tried to steady her breathing a bit.

"I'm thinking it's time to take off her bra, Shane."

"I completely agree."

Her breath hitched up in her throat. "Chilly, Sirs." It came out before she could stop herself.

Corey's fingers becoming instantly still and Shane's face tightening with concern made her wish she could take it back.

"Belle, tell us what you're feeling." Corey's gentle demand eased her anxiety a little.

Shane touched her cheek. "What do you need? Are we done?"

Done? No! "I just needed to catch my breath, Sir."

He nodded and touched her cheek. "What state are you in now, baby?"

She closed her eyes, taking stock of how she was feeling. Even though she was a little apprehensive, delicious tingles were also spreading through her.

Her two Doms wanted to show her off. They were proud of her. She never felt so beautiful in all her life. Yes, Shane and Corey were tough and dominant. They could be rough. They could push. They could demand. But underneath all the hardness was boundless goodness and love.

"I'm warm, Masters. Very warm."

Shane smiled. "Time to turn up the thermostat, sweetheart. Remove her bra, Corey. She's ready."

When the lace fell away from her breasts, Corey's large hands cupped them. He kneaded her mounds, and as promised, her temperature rose. Shane continued to stay right in front of her, screening her from the rest of the club.

He placed his hands on the small of her waist, just above her hips. "Lower your eyes."

She obeyed. "Yes, Master."

Corey rolled her nipples between his thumbs and forefingers, and she felt the pressure inside her expand as her tiny buds began to throb. "You are the most gorgeous woman in this place, Belle."

"No one can hold a candle to you, baby." Shane ran his fingers up and down her sides.

There were many beautiful women here. *Look at Paris.*

But the fact that Shane and Corey had told Belle she was the most beautiful made her feel so very sexy and adventurous. She was eager to let them show her off.

With her eyes still lowered, Shane removed her skirt. Now, she was completely naked, sandwiched between Shane and Corey. They were her only covering.

Corey kissed her neck. "What state are you in, sub?"

"Warm, Sir. Very warm."

Shane and Corey stepped back from her and moved to her sides. Her heart thudded in her chest, but she kept her eyes lowered, locking her gaze on the stilettos. The back of her knees softened, and if Shane and Corey hadn't held her by the elbows, she might've actually tumbled to the floor.

Corey's hand tightened just a little on her arm. "We'd like to present to you, the members of Phase Four, our sub, Belle."

She heard applause. Another wave of heat rolled through her as Shane and Corey turned her body around for all to see. She was shocked at how aroused this had made her. In fact, she enjoyed the attention the crowd was giving to her body. She could tell that Shane and Corey were very proud of her through all their tender touches. Never did their hands leave her.

They gently lifted her up and placed her on the table. Shane and Corey caressed her arms and legs. Out of the corner of her eye, she saw one of the cuffs attached to the table.

Are they going to place those on me? How would it feel to be restrained, unable to move, to be helpless and completely dependent on her two Doms? A tingle in her middle let her know she needed to find out, wanted to find out.

Shane leaned down over her. "What state are you in, baby?"

"Extremely warm, Master."

His smile thrilled her. He and Corey took her ankles and hands, locking them into the cuffs, which spread her out completely in the shape of an *X*.

When she felt the table turning, Corey said, "We want everyone to see our sub's beautiful pussy."

Shane bent down and said quietly, "Eyes on me and Corey only, understand?"

"Yes, Sir." *Oh my God, this is so much fun.* She was enjoying this more than she ever thought possible.

They adjusted the table to an angle that would give the onlookers the best view to her pussy. *Who knew I was such an exhibitionist?*

As the pressure multiplied inside her, the impulse to squeeze her thighs together to find any relief was so intense, but the cuffs wrapped around her ankles prevented her. So her suffering continued to grow and grow.

Corey's awe-filled words rumbled from deep in his chest. "Isn't this the most beautiful pussy you've ever seen?"

Another round of applause sent her to the moon and back. Her pussy dampened and she felt moisture dripping down her thighs.

"Who would like a closer look at our sweet sub's delicious, wet pussy?"

God, I just love this. I know I shouldn't but I do.

Men and women alike walked onto the platform.

Shane mouthed, "Eyes on me."

Belle nodded, though she could still see the crowd gathering around to admire her pussy in her peripheral vision. The *oohs* and *ahs* from this audience stoked her fire.

"Watch what happens when I touch her." And without hesitation, without giving her a second to get her head around his words, Shane put his hand on her pussy and spread her lips apart, letting the air hit her throbbing clit. He bent down and placed his mouth over her tiny bud, flicking it with his tongue. He leaned back and turned to the crowd. "See how much the sweet little thing has grown."

She heard positive exclamations from those present, which added to her excitement. *I'm so naughty. God, I love this, love being on display for my Doms.*

Corey leaned over her, and his handsome face filled her field of vision. Her pussy clenched on nothingness. She needed him and Shane to fill her body, to release the overwhelming pressure that was getting stronger and stronger by the second.

"Time to introduce our sub to fetish toys." He held up three little rubber-tipped clamps that were attached together by wires and plugged into a battery pack.

He licked both her nipples. Placing the clamps on her buds, he smiled.

The double bite of the toy instantly created a hot swirl that shot down to her pussy.

He held the third clamp, which was even smaller than the other two, in front of her eyes. "This little devil is going to blow our sub's mind."

When he clamped her clit with the thing, sparks fired all over her body, inside and out. The pressure was so powerful, so immediate, causing her need to shoot up faster and higher. If they didn't take her now, she was sure she wouldn't survive. "Please, Masters. Please."

"Hear that?" Shane laughed. "I will never tire of hearing my beautiful sub plead with me to end her suffering. But my brother and I are her Doms. We decide when she's had enough, not her. Us. Only us."

"But please, Sir. I need you so much."

"Yes, you do, sub." He grabbed one of the clamps on her nipples and tightened its hold, causing her heart to skip a beat.

"Oh God."

"Sub, you need Corey and me in every way, but we know about pleasure."

"It's our job to push your limits and to take you to places you never even dreamed possible." Corey kissed her forehead. "Brace yourself, baby. Let's turn on this little toy."

The clamps vibrated on her nipples and clit and she couldn't hold back her moans of surprise. The throbbing of her trio of buds was so immense, tears welled in her eyes.

Shane unfastened her ankles and placed a pillow under her, elevating her ass. He began applying lubricant, circling her tight ring with his fingers.

Corey turned the wicked device on and off, increasing the vibration to an insane level.

"Please. I can't stand much more." She didn't care who watched or who didn't. *Let the crowd go or let them stay.* Her pressure-filled passion could not be contained. "I need you, Masters. I need you so very much."

They both nodded. Corey removed the tiny clamps from her nipples and clit. As the blood returned to her little sensual buds, the burn and ache the clamps had left her was mind-blowing.

Through her lust-blurred vision, she watched them strip out of their leathers. *Yes. God. Yes.* Her pussy was soaked to the max. They took off the cuffs around her wrists. Corey lifted her off the table.

Shane stretched out on the table. "I want to feel that tight pussy around my cock, sub."

Corey guided her face down onto Shane.

She felt the head of Shane's cock press against her pussy.

Corey reached around and lightly stroked her clit, positioning his dick at the entrance to her ass.

"Please. Please. Please. Masters. I must have you inside me."

A wicked grin spread across Shane's face. "What state are you in, sub?"

Delirious with need and panting, she confessed, "I'm burning up inside, Sir. I'm on fire. Please. I beg you."

He nodded and thrust his cock deep into her pussy. Corey did the same in her ass. She screamed, uncaring who heard and unable to hold back.

As their dual, lusty plunges into her body picked up speed and intensity, the pressure hit a new level. She was so close. So very close.

The world seemed to melt away and all that was left were Shane and Corey, surrounding her with their dominance, their will, their love. In and out. Over and over.

Feeling that special spot get scratched thrust after thrust pushed her over the edge into a release that sent staggering sensations throughout her body. She felt tears of passion stream down her cheeks.

Shane and Corey groaned in unison, and she felt their cocks pulsing inside her body. Her pussy and ass clenched around their shafts again and again.

Riding out the scores of shivers, she heard their audience applaud.

Shane pressed his lips to her mouth and Corey kissed her neck.

Shane smiled. "You did great, baby."

"You sure did," Corey whispered from behind.

She grinned. "Are we supposed to take a bow, Masters?"

The both laughed.

Out of the corner of her eye, she saw the crowd exit the stage, leaving her alone with her wonderful men.

Shane kissed her again. "I'm so proud of you."

Corey stroked her hair. "Well, sweetheart, is this something you want to do again?"

"Please. Please. Please."

Again, they laughed and she joined in, glad that they'd kept their cocks inside her body.

This was where she belonged, between her two Doms.

* * * *

Shane gazed at Belle, who was lying on the bed between him and Corey. After leaving the club, they'd brought her back to the Boys Ranch, where they were staying for the time being.

The play had gone beyond what they'd planned. The more they gave her, the more she'd responded. There had been a special connection, a bond, a kind of union that he'd never experienced before. She was perfection in every sense of the word.

But did we push her too far tonight? After all, it was her first time at the club.

He looked over at his brother and could tell he was asking himself the same thing.

"What are you two thinking?" She smiled, her eyes so bright and full of life.

"The question is not what are *we* thinking." Shane stroked her hair. "It's what are *you* thinking, baby."

Corey traced her cheek with his fingers. "You're new to our lifestyle, Belle. Your first time can be exhausting and draining. How are you doing?"

"Me?" She giggled. "I'm fine. For me, my first time was not exhausting or draining."

"It wasn't?" Shane kissed her cheek.

"No. For me it was exhilarating and unbelievably wonderful. I am completely relaxed. There isn't an ounce of tension left in my body."

Shane grinned. He had never been happier in all his life. The night's play had been over-the-top incredible.

"When are we going back?"

"Look at our little sub, bro. She's anxious for more, and so am I."

"That makes three of us."

Corey kissed her until she moaned. He released her and leaned back on his elbow and looked into her eyes. "I love you, baby."

Before she could respond to his brother, Shane pressed his lips to Belle's. She was theirs now and forever. "I love you, Belle."

"I love you both so very much."

Chapter Twenty

Belle yawned.

"How was the club last night?" Amber grinned. "Seems like you might need a little more sleep."

"I'm fine." She smiled. "More than fine actually."

"I knew you would be."

"Three days until New Year's, Sis." Belle thought about Juan and Jake sleeping with the other boys in the dormitory. She, Juan, and Jake had spent Christmas night at Shane and Corey's house, but ever since, for the past two nights they'd all stayed here at the Boys Ranch. Their two wonderful sons didn't want to be far from their friends.

The place was nice and quiet. The sun was just coming up. She and Amber had been getting up earlier for several days. They loved their morning talks. "Won't the boys be shocked come New Year's day when the guys take them out on a secret dragon hunting expedition?"

"Yes, they will." Amber poured them two cups of coffee. She glanced out the window. "Who are your bodyguards this morning?"

"Shane and Corey, of course. It is strange to have a twenty-four seven detail around me at all times."

Her sister went back to the stove to tend the bacon and eggs she was preparing for them. "Well, it just has to be, Belle." Worry clouded Amber's face.

"Why don't I help you with breakfast, Sis?"

"I've got it, and stop trying to change the subject. Lunceford is ruthless. Until he's put away, you're going to have to get used to it."

"According to that creepy doctor Shannon's Elite captured in

Wyoming, Kip's disease is progressing. I might not have to wait long before he succumbs to his illness."

"We can only hope. The sooner that bastard is in the ground, the better."

"God, I never thought I'd feel that way about anyone, but I do."

Amber turned to her. "Shane and Corey and the rest of the town are going to make sure you stay safe."

She nodded. "I know."

"I'm glad that you and your guys decided to build a house here at the ranch. I like having you close."

"We had to. Moving Juan and Jake to town, even though it wasn't that far away, was out of the question. Besides, I think Shane and Corey like getting to help your guys teach all the boys about what it means to be a cowboy."

"I think you're right about that, Sis." Amber smiled. "It's good to see you so happy."

"I am happy. My life is so complete since the adoption has been finalized."

"That's obvious to me by the constant smile on your face, and I might add Shane and Corey's faces, too." Amber smiled and then her face turned white. "Oh no."

Belle leapt to her feet. "What's wrong?"

Her sister stepped back from the pan of bacon. "Just a little morning sickness. Smells activate it sometimes."

"Go sit down. I'll finish this." Belle took the spatula from Amber. "I knew I should've helped you. You're the pregnant one."

"Thanks."

Belle leaned over the stove and got a whiff of the bacon. Her stomach turned and she felt acid rise up in her throat. "Oh no. I must be having sympathy nausea. Where are the crackers?"

"That cabinet." Amber pointed to the one to the right of the stove. "The water is hot in the tea kettle. We can have tea and crackers for breakfast."

Belle nodded, holding her nose. She turned off the burner and grabbed a package of crackers. "This is crazy. My mind might be past the kidnapping but my stomach certainly isn't."

"Has this happened before, Belle?"

She nodded. "Once right after they rescued me and a few times after that."

Amber started laughing.

"Why are you laughing at me being sick, Sis?" She bit into a cracker, hoping it would settle her upset stomach.

"Because I think you're pregnant."

"Amber, don't get my hopes up for that. I'm happy. I have Juan and Jake. The guys want to adopt more children. It's enough."

"It may be enough, but it's my duty as your little sister to help you find out." Amber stood. "And we're going to do that right now."

"Right now?"

"Yes. I have a pregnancy test I didn't use. Actually, I have two left. I had three. When I missed my period, all three of them brought one home for me." She laughed. "I love those three nuts."

Belle tried to quell the excitement that Amber was stoking. "I can't be, Sis. You know that."

The little firecracker put her hands on her hips. "I'm going to give you two choices. One, I take you in my bathroom and you pee on a stick. Two, I call Doc and get him to schedule you an upper and lower GI test. Which will it be?"

"I guess you've got me. Let's get this over with." Following Amber to the bathroom, Belle counted the days since her last period. She was a week late, but kept that to herself, not wanting to fuel Amber's excitement. *It can't be.* She reminded herself that her cycle had never been regular like her sister's, just another thing her disease had caused.

Amber opened up the cabinet and brought out the two pregnancy tests. She opened one and handed her the stick. "Pee on this."

Belle squatted over the toilet and urinated on the stick. Her heart thudded in her chest as she fixed her stare to the result area. Amber peered over her shoulder. They remained frozen in position for what seemed like an eternity.

"Oh my God, Belle. It's positive."

"This can't be right. This must be faulty. Give me another one."

"You're kidding, right? You're a nurse. You know how rare it is for these tests to be positive unless they are positive. You have a better chance of being struck by lightning on a clear day."

She shook her head. "Hand it over." After drowning the remaining pregnancy test with her pee, Belle realized the impossible had happened. "I'm pregnant, Amber."

Her sister hugged her. "That's what I've been trying to tell you, Sis." She winked. "I guess I am the smart one."

"Oh my God, I can't believe it. Should I go lie down?"

Amber laughed. "You're the one who worked in a maternity ward. You tell me?"

Her eyes welled up. "I'm just so happy. I love being sick."

Tears rolled down Amber's face. "Me, too."

My dream has finally come true. "Dream? Pinch me, Sis. Tell me this isn't a dream."

"It's real, Belle." Amber grabbed a little of her arm's flesh.

"Ouch. It is real." She kissed her sister on the cheek. "We're going to have babies together."

"Stay here, Belle. I'll be right back." Amber ran out of the bathroom.

"Are you still sick?"

No answer. Was she going to get them crackers? Belle's stomach was settling down.

She couldn't stop looking at the tiny stick in her hand.

She heard footsteps headed her way.

Shane and Corey appeared at the door.

"Baby, are you okay?" Shane reached over and wiped a tear from her cheek. "Amber said to come right away."

Corey grabbed her hand. "What's wrong, sweetheart?"

"It's just…just so…I am…" She couldn't get the words out, so she held up the stick. "I peed on this. Look."

Realization came over both her guys' faces.

Shane spoke first. "You mean?"

Corey smiled. "Really?"

She nodded.

They both picked her up, showering her in kisses. They spun her around in circles in the tiny bathroom.

Suddenly, they stopped.

Shane's eyes widened. "Oh my God, should you lie down, Belle?"

"How about a cold cloth?" Corey touched her cheek.

Amber appeared at the doorway with her three husbands. "We've been through that already, fellas. She'll be fine. She's just pregnant."

"Just?" Shane laughed. "This is the happiest day in my life."

"Mine, too," Corey chimed in.

The three Stone brothers stepped forward, congratulating them.

"Okay, men." Amber smiled. "This isn't that big of a bathroom. Let's let the mother-to-be have a moment with her guys. Besides, I need you to finish cooking breakfast."

"Are you okay, baby?" Emmett asked, putting his arm around Amber's shoulder.

"I just didn't know bacon could smell like that, honey." Amber turned to her. "Trust me, Sis. Doms are always overprotective, but when you're pregnant, doubly so. That's something you'll have to get used to besides the queasiness."

"I love you, Sis."

"I love you, too." Amber nodded and her men left.

Corey pressed his mouth tenderly to hers. "Are you queasy now?"

"No."

Shane kissed her so gently. "Can I get you a glass of water?"

She laughed. "And so it starts. No. I'm fine. Better than fine. I'm so happy. Thank you."

Her dreams of having a baby had come true. She was already a mother with two sweet boys, who she loved so very much and who also had two amazing dads in Corey and Shane. Her life was better than she'd ever imagined, and it was all because of her wonderful men.

"I love you both so very much."

Corey squeezed her hand. "I love you, sweetheart."

"And I love you, too, baby." Shane turned to Corey. "Let's carry our girl to the kitchen."

Corey nodded and lifted her up in his arms.

"I'm pregnant, guys." She smiled. "My legs still work just fine."

THE END

WWW.CHLOELANG.COM

ABOUT THE AUTHOR

Born in Missouri, I am happy to call Dallas, Texas, home, now. Who doesn't love sunshine?

I began devouring romance novels during summers between college semesters as a respite to the rigors of my studies. Soon, my lifelong addiction was born, and to this day, I typically read three or four books every week.

For years, I tried my hand at writing romance stories, but shared them with no one. Understand, I'm really shy. After many months of prodding by friends, author Sophie Oak, I finally relented and let them read one. As the prodding turned to gentle shoves, I ultimately did submit something to Siren-BookStrand. The thrill of a life happened for me when I got the word that my book would be published.

I do want to warn the reader that my books are not for the faint of heart, and are strictly for adults. That said, I love erotic romances. Blending the sexual chemistry with the emotional energy between the characters in my books is why I love being a writer.

For all titles by Chloe Lang, please visit
www.bookstrand.com/chloe-lang

Siren Publishing, Inc.
www.SirenPublishing.com

CPSIA information can be obtained at www.ICGtesting.com
Printed in the USA
LVOW04s0506031214

416755LV00031B/1652/P